INTO THE LIGHT

KATIE-LOUISE MERRITT

Published by Lyvit Publishing, Cornwall

www.lyvit.com

ISBN 978-0-9926029-9-4

DEDICATION

For my grandchildren & great grandchildren

Matthew, Nicolette, Lucy and Harley
Dylan, Oliver and Lowen,
My pearls of love.

And for Richard, my brother, with love

Chapter One

Singapore 1940

I DID NOT know it then but my destiny began on a ship, a quirk of fate which like the flip of a coin can change the course of one's life.

She stood at our side on the ship's deck, slender and neatly dressed in cool cream linen; a woman in her late thirties with light brown hair pulled back into a chignon. She smiled politely and formally introduced herself as we turned from watching the shores of Malaya recede from view and our ship embrace a vast expanse of sea and sky, unlike anything I had ever seen before.

'How do you do. I'm Verity Nicholls,' she said.

My mother, lifting me down from the ship's rail, took her outstretched hand.

'Pleased to meet you,' she replied, 'I'm Faith Johnson.'

The lady looked down at me with a sadness concealed from the world behind pale blue eyes. 'And what's your name?' she asked with an imperceptible gesture of her hand as if to touch my hair.

I took a step closer to my mother.

'This is Madeline,' Faith replied, with an encouraging smile at me to say "Hello." 'We're going home aren't we for you to meet your Granny and Granddad?'

I nodded, shyly.

'My parents live in London, in Tottenham,' she continued. 'Not the best time or place to be visiting my parents with a war on, but life has to go on, doesn't it? …..Whatever surprises it may throw at you,' she added.

Verity agreed and if she had wondered at my mother's ambiguous aside, she gave no indication but gazed down at me and I saw in her face a look of intense yearning. 'Your parents will be enchanted with her. She's beautiful. How old is she?'

'She's just gone two. When we get home, I daresay there will be a surprise party arranged for everyone to meet her. We're a tribe that loves an excuse for a knees-up,' she said, grinning at the memory, 'and Madeline will be a wonderful reason for us all to get together and Hitler can do his damndest!'

On board ship I watched their friendship grow. Unalike in temperament and dress, they seemed drawn to each other by their very dissimilarities. My mother, safe in my tender years, confided in me her thoughts and impressions of the people she had met as she prepared me for bed in artificial light. It was hot and sticky in the cabin with the porthole blacked out to prevent not a chink of us to be seen by enemy gun boats.

'Some of them are rather snooty, Madeline, and think themselves better than everyone else, like that awful piggy-eyed woman,' she said, comically puffing out her cheeks and screwing up her eyes at me, 'and her daughter has hair that looks as if it's been cut around a pudding basin!' She pulled a shock of her curls straight down the sides of her face and scowled like the daughter, and we chortled together like two naughty children.

With an intake of breath she became serious and said, 'Now, Verity Nicholls is different. She has a kind and gentle way. One of the old school where good manners and tradition are the pillars of her life, and with a place for everything and everything in its place! Not like your untidy, mum!' she said, with a tickling of my ribs and another peal of laughter. She slipped me into my nightdress. 'Come on then, into bed with you,' and pushing back a thick curtain of chestnut-red hair from her face, she knelt to kiss me goodnight. I reached out to play with her hair for I loved to watch the corkscrew curls bouncing back and she smiled with a soft faraway look and said my touch reminded her of daddy.

My mother's free spirit and her ability to engage people I saw had a startling effect on the passengers. Initially responding, trapped as they were on the confines of a passenger cargo ship and not unaware of the danger we collectively faced through waters patrolled by German U boats, they nevertheless quickly retreated into tightly held British reserve, keeping their distance from this unconventional woman whose pale olive skin hinted at foreign blood, and whose hair fell free from restricting pins and sausage curl style of the day into a mass of spiralling tendrils.

Faith felt the subtle closing of ranks, and Verity observing their withdrawal, shook her head at the straight jacket of the Colonial system. 'You may depend these people come from quite ordinary backgrounds. I've met their sort before and their behaviour does not endear me to our fellow countrymen.'

'What's life like in Kuala Lumpur, Mrs. Nicholls?' asked Faith, on what would become a routine morning stroll together along the deck before taking coffee in the lounge.

'Please, do call me Verity.'

Faith was taken by surprise. To suggest the informality of her Christian name in such a short time of acquaintance was unusual, and from someone whom she had observed was of a retiring nature.

'Unlike some of the women, I took to life in KL like a duck to water,' she went on. 'It's so vibrant with the different nationalities living and working in the city. Maurice, my husband, is a civil servant and through him I've met the wives of the men in the various departments of the administrative offices. We meet up to play bridge and mahjong, or take shopping trips into China town. Their gold shops are quite amazing with displays of gold and jade guarded by a Sikh outside holding a gun, would you believe, as there are no doors, just iron gates which close at night; the wives coffee mornings I do my best to avoid. Instead I take lessons in Chinese painting and Ikebana.'

'Ikebana? What's that? I've never heard of it.'

'It's Japanese flower arranging with the idea of nature and humanity being linked together in simple lines of arrangement. The spiritual aspect is also very important. It's not as easy as it sounds as everything has to be harmonious using maybe a couple of pieces of wood and a flower or two. It's completely different from our English way of arranging flowers.'

'I don't think that would be my cup of tea at all. My flower arranging is a bit haphazard. I plonk them in a vase and let them fall where they will.......' Faith stopped abruptly, distracted by my slipping her hand to run to one of the ships bollards which I began to climb.

Her slim legs ate up the length of the deck as she came running after me and hauled me off squirming to be let down.

Verity caught us up laughing. 'She's so quick!'

'I know. I can't take my eyes off her for a minute,' Faith apologized.

'So I see! Shall we go in for an early coffee and a drink for Madeline? It will take her mind off climbing.'

'Good idea,' Faith agreed. 'The trouble is her freedom is rather restricted on board with the capstans

4

and deck fittings, and she could slip under the protective canvas on the railings in the blink of an eye,' she said, as they went down a deck to the lounge and settled themselves in tub chairs gathered around a coffee table.

A Eurasian waiter came over quickly to them for their orders. 'I like him he's always so pleasant and efficient,' Faith observed, as he went off. 'I hope you won't mind me asking, but I was wondering why your husband isn't with you?'

'It's because his leave isn't due until the end of the year. It would have been such a help to have had him with me as my mother is ill in hospital with a stroke. It's the reason I'm going home. My father died some years ago, and as an only child born late in their lives, I have no siblings who could keep an eye on her recovery which in the nature of strokes could be a long time.'

'I'm so sorry to hear of your mother,' said Faith with sympathy. 'It must be difficult with no-one to turn to.'

'Yes, it is rather. I'll just have to wait and see what the situation is when I arrive in Surrey.'

'I can't imagine what it's like having no brothers or sisters,' Faith mused. 'I've two of each and with so many of us there was the constant noise of kids squabbling and never a corner to call my own. I was the youngest and shared a bedroom with my sisters. They used to drive me crazy. Bunny is a night owl. She came to bed like a herd of elephants, switching on the lights, opening and shutting drawers and generally thumping around, and Jess is an early bird who wakes up full of the joys of spring and chatter. Bunny's late nights never seemed to bother Jess, she was dead to the world, but I used to go about in a permanent haze as a teenager from disturbed nights. I'm not convinced it didn't have dire consequences on my development!'

Verity grinned. 'Oh what a calamity!' pulling a comical face at me, and I bit my lip to hide a smile.

Faith rose from her chair, 'Before the coffee arrives, I'll just go and fetch Madeline's doll and tea set from the cabin. She loves to play tea parties with her. 'Madeline, will you be a good girl and stay here with Aunt Verity for a minute. I'm going to get Rosie for you.' She hesitated, expecting a protest for I had clung to her for days after finding myself uprooted from my home and father in Malaya, but to her surprise I slid down from my chair to sit beside Verity, presenting her with one of my biggest sunshine smiles, as Faith called them. Her sad eyes brightened as if I had given her a prize and she put her arm around me.

On Faith's return I knelt up at the coffee table and began laying out my tea set. Their conversation drifted to Faith's life outstation.

'The silly thing is that now I would give anything for the mad hurly-burly of our family. I've found it hard, the loneliness on a plantation with only the trees for company. Our nearest neighbour is miles away and Roger might as well be as I see so little of him. He's out on the rubber plantation by the ungodly hour of five o'clock in the morning, instructing his work crews, examining trees for any disease to be eradicated and checking equipment. After breakfast he's off to the factory and after lunch he's in the office catching up on paper work or he's at meetings. In the evenings he likes a drink or two and slopes off to bed early unless we meet up with friends for a rubber of bridge.' Faith sighed. 'He's more than ten years older than me, so it was a well established routine as a bachelor before we met, and, I soon discovered, a way of life with rubber planters.'

'Your day does sound rather a lonely one,' Verity sympathized, pouring the coffee that had arrived at the table. She handed a cup to Faith and turning to me said, 'I'm playing at being mum today, Madeline. Would you like your orange juice? You can give some to Rosie too,' pouring a little into my toy milk jug for me. 'Are there no clubs in the area where you could meet other women?' she asked, sitting back and sipping her coffee.

'Yes, there's the seventh mile club where the wives of planters and miners and their families congregate for a swim during the week and for a curry tiffin at weekends, but the club is so crowded it takes time to get to know people and the women can be clicky.' Faith chuckled. 'There's one chap who's very popular and holds court with the most hilarious anecdotes. He's certainly no oil painting with his beer belly and looks rather like a monk with his receding hair, but he has that attractive trait in a man of making a woman laugh. A magnetism that is unmistakable. There's no accounting for attraction is there? It can strike when you least expect it.' Her smile faded, her eyes shying away from something unspoken, and she stared into her coffee cup.

'I'm sorry Verity, I must sound like the biggest moaner on earth. I do have one friend, called Judith, who lives on another plantation. We link up from time to time, taking in turns for our houses. I'm very envious of her swimming pool where we cool off before having our lunch. She's an expert bridge player, much better than her husband actually, and I've learnt a lot from her when Roger and I enjoy a rubber with them once a week.' She paused, thinking.

'Talking of bridge. If we could find another couple on board who enjoy a game, perhaps we could play a rubber or two of an evening? What do you think? It would help to pass the time,' Faith said.

Verity agreed. 'I'll ask the Purser to put a notice up. There must be a few on board who are willing to put aside protocol and be glad to forget for a while we are sailing in dangerous waters.'

With our ship unable to pass through the Suez Canal, we navigated across the Indian Ocean to Cape Town and from there hugged the coast of West Africa to Liberia where we waited to rendezvous with a convoy of ships for the relative protection of sailing together through the Atlantic Ocean. On the convoy failing to appear, our captain told us, to a shiver of apprehension that rolled around the ship like a wave, he had taken the decision to go it alone in a wide zigzag course across the Atlantic. We would be sailing as far as Greenland to avoid the U boats prowling off Ireland, and with good luck and God speed we would safely dock in Glasgow.

The ship cast off once more and Faith and Verity were resolute and determined to put a mental best foot forward. The days and weeks passed until it seemed I had always lived on board ship with my mother and Verity with our daily routine of boat drills and constant reminders that we had only minutes to get to our specific life boat station and be lowered to the water if struck by a torpedo. There seemed to be an unspoken easing of formalities from the majority of passengers; bridge was arranged for the evenings, and deck games were played in teams during the day. Verity and Faith passed the time easy in each other's company; laughing together when they attempted to play shuffleboard with the ship rolling from side to side with a turbulent sea. I saw them cleverly judge the motion of the waves, waiting for the ship to level out before a quick push of the wooden discs with a long cue towards the numbered scoring sections marked on the deck. We played deck quoits where I was gently pushed forward to stand close to the solid wooden base and squealing with delight at my success when one of my wild throws of a quoit landed over the pole. I raced to retrieve ping-pong balls for them when they flew off the tennis table and bounced them around under the noses of the passengers, giggling back at Faith's barely hidden grin. When tiring of playing deck games, we cooled off in the small canvas sided pool, or spread out on chairs beneath awnings shading us from the fierce heat, and I would sit, more often than not, in Verity's lap listening to the murmuring of their voices. It was then I heard her say she had had a miscarriage and was told it was highly unlikely she would able to have another child. She had hoped against hope the gynaecologist was wrong, but it seemed he was right for they hadn't been blessed again so far, and time was not on her side, she said, her eyes bright with tears. She pulled me gently to her and I drifted to sleep, lulled with the hypnotic throb of the engines and the wash of the sea.

As we drew closer to England I shivered with the unexpected cool sea air. Where was the sun? I missed its warmth on my skin and I missed daddy too. The sea became choppy spraying wide over the bows of the ship and the high and mighty turned delightful shades of green and disappeared one by one to their cabins. Smugly we celebrated our sea-legs, eating our meals in an empty dining room to the sight of the sea rising to starboard to the height of the windows, only to crash down again, and up the port side. After we'd eaten, we lurched along the corridors to our cabins, like three drunken men, where safely tucked up in my bunk bed and a story read, I could stay awake no longer, rocked to sleep in the cradle of the waves.

'Wake up, sweetheart,' cried my mother one morning and she hastily dressed me with an air of excitement. 'Today we are leaving the ship and soon you will be seeing your granny and granddad, and I must pack up our things.'

Our captain had, against all the odds, brought us safely to the Glasgow docks. That evening walking down the gang plank I recoiled with the shock of a day coloured grey and with a bitterly cold wind. The quayside was full of noise and confusion with uniformed men and armoury in transit from all parts of the country, bringing forcibly home to us England was at war.

Verity hunkered down and held me close, her eyes holding mine with a smile that could not conceal her sadness at our parting.

'Be a good girl now, for mummy.'

I slipped my arms around her neck breathing in her familiar smell of rose scented soap mingling with her fresh lemony hair. She stood, and we all felt a sharp sense of loss for the peaceful oasis of our friendship on board ship. Verity and Faith hugged each other tightly and we parted into a world fragmented by war.

Chapter Two

THE REUNION WAS, as my mother predicted, a large and noisy affair in a room crowded with her friends and relations. I was submerged in demonstrations of their love and exclamations at my strawberry-blond hair, my wide grey green eyes, the family likeness with my Jewish nose, distinct, but not overtly so, and observing that they could see little of my father in me. I responded to their welcome with shyness and ran to my mother, longing to be away from these strange people and back on the ship to the sound of the sea and the murmuring voices of Verity and Faith sitting on deck in the heat-held days.

My mother good humouredly reproached them. 'You're frightening her half to death! She's not used to a noisy tribe like us. On the plantation it's only you, me and daddy, isn't it Madeline? And of course, Janita our amah,' she added with a frown. She kissed me and I nodded and buried my face into her shoulder and stayed there, close to her body and the sweet perfume of Evening in Paris.

I grew to love my grandparents who lived in London in a long row of terraced houses in Tottenham where the backs overlooked a railway line and where, to my amazement, from my bedroom window I could see the most wonderful thing, a great silver balloon that floated and yet never moved from my sight.

Owen, my grandfather, was short in height and sinewy with a head of curly jet black hair. He walked with a limp that threw his body out of kilter from a hip

11

that had been pinned as a child on contracting infantile paralysis. He pulled my leg with all the blarney of his heritage, enchanting me with stories of the leprechauns that lived in his garden before the family moved to England and I never tired of hearing of the wee Irish faerie folk that were mischievous and liked to play tricks on people. Taking me onto his lap, his voice close to my ear, he spun his tales.

'Not everyone can see them, Madeline but I could! They were smartly dressed in green suits with bright red or yellow waistcoats, and on their feet they wore buckled shoes. They were so small, they could sit on my shoulder and at night, I would sneak into the garden to watch them play their tin whistles, harps and drums. They would dance to their music all night long and drink moonshine which made them very drunk and talkative. One night I heard them chattering excitedly about hidden treasure; a big hoard of golden coins! Now times were hard for my mother and father, and I knew if I could find it, we wouldn't have to move away from my home and my friends. Well, I hunted and hunted for it, and dug holes all over our vegetable patch which did not please my da at all.'

I was captivated at the thought of buried golden coins.

But then he sighed and said, 'I never found any, my little *bubbula*, so we had to leave Ireland and come to seek our fortune here.'

My grandmother, Ruth, round as a dumpling, lifted her eyes from darning his socks with a look of dry amusement, and scolded him for talking such nonsense to a child.

In reply, he winked at me and pulled a funny face and I giggled in glee.

His words rolled off his tongue with all the lilt of the Irish,

'Ah, to be sure, don't you believe your old grandmother. Every word I've spoken is the gospel truth!'

'And less of the *old*, my cock sparrow!' retorted my grandmother.

Granddad's eyes were teasing. 'When I met your grandmother, she was the sweetest little thing I'd ever set eyes on. She was an angel who appeared at my bedside when I was a young man and poorly in hospital. "Do you fancy a cup of tea?!" she said, looking down at me with eyes as blue as the sky and looking as pretty as a picture in her nurse's uniform. "I can see more than a cup of tea to fancy, I told her!" and she laughed, and I fell in love with her that very moment.'

My grandmother hushed him with a look that suppressed a smile. 'Enough of all this moonshine talk. She's just a baby!'

He grinned broadly at her, 'Righty-ho, my little plum duff!'

He ruffled my hair and setting me down, lifted his tin hat and first aid bag that hung on the back door. 'Well, time to be off,' he called out.

Faith turned her head, her hands resting on the rim of the stone sink, soapy from washing my dresses. I watched in fascination the droplets sliding down the sink and cupboard beneath to drip in bubbles onto the floor.

'Take care, dad,' she said, with an anxious look, for there were times when he disappeared for days on air raid patrol and this was to be no different.

On the verge of exhaustion, he returned home three days later, his face streaked white and grey with dust, his deep treacle brown eyes dulled.

'We pulled children out today, Ruth,' and then said no more at my watchful face. He sat down wearily and

I could smell smoke on his navy-blue uniform, like the bonfires he made in the garden.

I lifted my arms to sit on his lap and turning, placed my hands around his face. 'Granddad tired,' I said.

'Don't you fret, my little *bubbula*. Just to see you with your golden hair like the morning sun makes me feel on top of the world!'

Pleased, I smiled at him. 'Stories!'

'You shall have a story but first granddad must have a good wash, then we'll have our tea, and after that when you're tucked up in bed, I'll tell you another tale of those mischievous leprechauns.'

Later, I heard him say, 'You know Ruth, it could be my imagination, but I really do feel so much better when the little one is around me. She brings to mind my grandmother who had the gift of healing.'

Fear came suddenly one night with a terrifying wail of a siren over our long street of houses. My mother pulling me from sleep, raced me to the running damp and cold of our Anderson shelter where my grandfather ingeniously grew vegetables on its roof, and where we lay trying to ignore the drone of planes overhead, the ground-shaking thump and crunch of bombs, the sound of shrapnel tinkling down the roofs. I drew close to my mother and fretted as to why she had brought me to such a cold and horrible place.

'Hush, sweetheart. You must try and sleep,' my mother whispered, holding me as two spoons lying tightly together.

On venturing out the next morning to the corner shop which had defied destruction, we stumbled along, picking our way through bricks and masonry of houses in smoking ruins, and dodging little fountains of water from burst mains. I looked up in astonishment at a house open to the skies and road, its front blasted away leaving pictures askew on the walls. A broken mirror hung amongst wallpaper hanging in strips, and two horses and a clock stood on the mantel of a kitchen range with its oven door gaping open. Upstairs, a bed tilting at a crazy angle hung half-balanced over the remains of a floor. On following my gaze Faith's face creased with anger.

'A bad man sent his planes to do that. He likes to kill people - especially Jews,' she spoke under her breath.'

But I caught her words and was, at that moment, possessed of a terror greater than the menacing wail of the siren and the drone of planes dropping their bombs. I had a Jewish nose. Aunt Jessie said so and seeing my face crumple in fear, she crouched down holding me close in a flurry of self-reproach.

'Oh sweetheart, I'm sorry, I didn't mean to frighten you. You will always be safe with me and your granny and granddad,' she said, looking earnestly into my face. 'You know that don't you?'

'Yes,' I nodded, fearful still as I looked around me at the broken houses.

We carried on to the shop and came upon a young boy and a girl sitting on a battered settee on the pavement drinking tea provided by the Salvation Army, whilst their mother salvaged what little she could from the remains of their home. My mother stopped and asked her if the children were alright and if they had anywhere to stay. She replied the children were shaken up, and she hoped they would be able to bunk down for the time being with a friend of hers.

'My Ernie is in for a shock,' the woman said, gazing at the devastation of their home. We were lucky not to take a direct hit like poor Mrs. Jones at number twenty six who was killed outright when taking a bath. She was blown, bath and all, into the garden.'

Faith was horrified. 'Oh the poor soul. What happened to her little dog?'

'No-one's seen him, He might have been killed or just run away,' the woman replied.

Faith looked down anxiously at me at this talk of death and made a move for us to walk on. 'Well, I hope you have success with your friend. Good luck.'

'Thanks, me duck.'

Faith was quiet and preoccupied on continuing down the road and it was not until she heard Mr. Jackson, our grocer, expanding on the latest antics of his nephews to an amused audience of his customers, that her spirits lifted and she grinned to herself every now and then as we walked back home.

'We shall have to tell your granny and granddad about Mr. Jackson's naughty nephews won't we? It will cheer them up.'

At tea-time, sitting around the table, I was hungry and waited impatiently for my egg to boil and could think of nothing but the pleasure of dipping my bread into the yoke and eating it. I had soon learnt that food was not plentiful in this country of cold and fear that came out of the skies wreaking havoc and devastation. It was rationed, my mother told me. I watched her spread thinly her ration of butter onto my bread and cut it into fingers. A smile hovered around her mouth.

'Mr. Jackson was telling us about the latest escapades of his nephews Danny and Jeff - typical boys with too much imagination for their own good by the sound of it. Apparently, God knows how, they got their hands on some petrol, splashed it around an old dustbin with holes in it and a wonky lid, wrapped a cloth around a piece of stick, set fire to it, stuck it through one of the holes, and *boom* the lid shot up into the air! They were having a whale of a time until a bobby on the beat put a stop to it and sent them packing! You have to give it to them, it was ingenious really. The things those two get up to, it's a wonder they don't blow themselves to kingdom come.'

She grinned. 'The latest stunt was frightening half-to-death their neighbour Mr. Mellor, a nervous, inoffensive little man constantly worried by the rumours of invasion. He was quietly getting on digging away to make an Anderson shelter when all of a sudden a gun appeared through a hole in his fence above him and a voice ordered him to 'stick 'em up!' Startled out of his wits, he threw down his shovel, leaped out of the ground, and ran hell-for-leather down the garden path into his house and slammed the door shut. Mr. Jackson's sister saw it all from her upstairs window and was laughing as much as the boys who were falling around cuffing and punching each other in glee at the wondrous sight of Mr. Mellor's flying exit from his garden! It had gone better than they could ever have imagined, until his wife Violet, built like a battleship with a voice to match, made a rapid appearance at the back gate. Mr. Jackson's sister said anyone less like the flower she was named after you'd be hard put to find, and if you valued your life, you didn't mess with Violet and that included any Germans thinking they might take a pop at her husband. Danny and Jeff showing a clean pair of heels skittered away down the lane and roared home, convulsed in giggling silliness. The next thing they knew, there was as a loud knocking at the door with the arrival of Violet with Mr. Mellor who was getting more worked up by the minute at the thought of being hoodwinked by a couple of kids.'

'Your boys shouldn't be allowed to play with guns, and go around pointing them at people. I ought to report you. It frightened the wits out of me and my wife,' he ranted.

'If the Boche met Violet, the war would be over!' Jeff breathed to Danny.

His mother gave Jeff a warning look whilst barely containing her own splutter of laughter. 'It was only a broken air gun Mr. Mellor,' she explained, stopping him in full flow, and wondering why Violet, who would fight herself if she could, was strangely quiet.

'Well.....even so,' he grunted, 'it was a very stupid thing to do in these dangerous times with all the talk of invasion.'

For the sake of peace, she agreed, and made the boys apologize.

'Honestly!' Faith exclaimed. 'What a fuss over two little boys playing at soldiers and I wonder why Violet was so quiet?'

'There for back-up, I dare say. She probably loaded the gun and left her husband to fire it!' replied Owen, chortling at his own pun. 'Still, whilst it has its funny side, I have a certain amount of sympathy for Mr. Mellor,' he said, pouring everyone a cup of tea. 'Boys are attracted to danger like the proverbial to the fan. I find it the devil's own job keeping them away from bomb sites and houses with walls ready to cave in as they root around for pieces of shrapnel from exploded anti-aircraft shells, cone heads, and those strips of 'chaff' to confuse the radar of bombers, and any other bits and pieces of war memorabilia they can find to build up a collection and do swops with their friends.'

'Well, that's boys for you,' Ruth said, lifting the egg from the boiling water and dropping it into my beautiful hen-shaped egg cup.

Simultaneously, the house rocked and vibrated. In slow motion, I watched granny's family photos and her favourite vases crash from the mantelpiece onto the floor. In disbelief, I saw the windows shatter and blow out in shards and my egg disappeared into a thick cloud of dust and broken plaster that rained down on us from the ceiling.

'My egg! My egg!' I screamed, for only the egg cup remained.

With her face as white as our clothes covered in dust, Faith came and took me into her arms. 'It's alright, sweetheart, It's alright. You can have one another day.'

I pulled myself away from her hold. 'I don't want another one. I want this one. I want my egg! I want my egg!' I howled, and burst into tears.

'I've never known her to act like this,' said Faith, forcing me tightly to her, her face taut with fear.

Ruth tried to pacify me. 'Don't you cry my little *bubbala*. Granny's here. Those nasty planes have all gone now and like mummy told you, you can have another egg soon,' she said, attempting to take pieces of plaster from my hair. But I was sobbing and beyond reason and on sharply turning my head away from her, she gave up, and leaving Faith to calm me down, began to clear the mess from the table.

'She's in shock, that's what it is,' said Owen, fetching the broom from under the stairs and began sweeping the debris from the floor into a heap.

As my tears subsided, our next door neighbour came running in. 'Is everyone all right? I heard the little one screaming.' Her eyes took in the damage to the ceiling. 'We were lucky. The blast missed us.'

'Madeline's upset because her egg just vanished, leaving only the egg cup, Mrs. Pearce,' said Faith. 'Would you believe it?'

'Now, hush, don't you fret, little one,' soothed Mrs. Pearce. 'I have an egg. Shall we take your lovely chicken egg cup into my house and give it a wash, and whilst your granddad and granny are clearing up this mess, I'll cook another egg.'

'I couldn't possibly take your egg ration, Mrs. Pearce,' said Faith.

'Nonsense. It will help Madeline to get over the shock. The experience must have been terrifying for her.'

'Well, it really is most kind of you but you must let me replace it next week.'

Mrs. Pearce led us out and into the normality of a clean and tidy home and taking me to the kitchen sink she ran the tap and before I knew it was briskly rubbing my face and hands with a wet flannel.

'Now, that feels better already doesn't it? You just sit down at the table and before you can say Humpty Dumpty, the egg will be ready!' Faith surprised as I was at the speed in which we were taken in hand, sat me down and parked herself beside me.

Mrs. Pearce bustled around, cutting a slice of bread into soldiers, and eager to share with a new audience the full horror stories of the blitz began to tell us how wonderful our brave young men were during the battle of Britain when she had watched the dog fights overhead. She rattled on whilst we waited for the egg to boil and I saw my mother's warning stare at her with a slight shake of her head. She stopped, abruptly, glancing between us.

'I'm so sorry, my dear. Me and my big mouth,' she flustered, scooping the egg out of the saucepan and placing it before me.

'You mustn't take any notice of me, Madeline. I'm just a silly old woman. Now, eat up and by the time you've finished, your granny and granddad will have the mess all cleared up.'

Ruth and Owen had taken the bomb blast with the stoic acceptance of all bomb weary Londoners. Owen repaired the windows, the ceiling was re-plastered and our routine of life carried on but Faith was unsettled and on edge until the day a letter arrived from Verity. It brought the sad news of her mother, who, shortly after being taken into a nursing home, had developed pneumonia and died. She was still in a state of shock, she wrote, and felt the need to get away from her parent's home and had taken a train to their holiday cottage in Penzance. She was wondering if we would like to come and visit, adding, we could stay as long as we wished.

Faith's sympathy was matched by her elation at the chance to leave London. She scooped me up, dancing us around the room. 'You'd like to see Verity again wouldn't you sweetheart? She lives by the sea!'

We waltzed and swayed together, overjoyed at the thought of seeing Verity. I had missed her, and something within me knew that when we came it would make her happy. My world was bright again, until the thought of leaving my grandparents. Granddad had said I made him feel better. Couldn't they come with us?

Breathless from dancing, Faith set me down. 'No, they won't be able to do that, Madeline. They have always lived here and you know that Granddad is an air warden and has a very important job to do to keep people safe, just like I must keep you safe for daddy.'

I was downcast.

She cuddled me to her. 'I know this is another move from people you love, and who love you, but this time, we shall stay with Verity until the end of this horrible war is over. I promise.'

That evening, there was laughter when Owen related to us the tale he'd heard from a warden who on entering a perilous state of a house found an old woman rooting around in what was left of her bedroom.

'Come on, Missus, get a move on!' he urged her. 'This building is ready to collapse at any moment.'

"I'm not leaving this house without me corsets on; I never 'ave an' never will. 'Itler can go to hell! Bombing innocent people in their beds! I ain't shifting until they're on, and you can turn your back an' all!' she said and proceeded to haul them over her ample flesh.

On their laughter dying away, my mother took the opportunity to break the news to them.

'I've had a letter from Verity. She has invited Madeline and me to stay in Cornwall for as long as we like and I've decided we should go.'

'This is a bit sudden isn't it, Faith?' my grandmother said.

'Actually, mum, I've been thinking about it for some time now after the air raid when so many houses were destroyed on this street, and that day when our whole house shook with bomb blast. I was terrified. I knew then it was time to leave. This invitation from Verity is a heaven sent opportunity.'

My grandmother, although crestfallen, agreed. 'You're right, of course dear, I'm being selfish. It's just that I've got used to having you around again and getting to know our new granddaughter. She is my little *bubbala*,' she laughed, hugging me to her bosom as we sat together on the sofa, and then whispered, 'that means little darling, and that's what you are to your granddad and me.' She sighed. 'Dad and I will miss her.'

'Yes, we will but I agree entirely with your decision to go to Cornwall,' said Owen. 'The blast shook us all up and we would never forgive ourselves if either of you came to any harm. The most important thing is your safety.'

'Thanks dad. I knew you'd both understand. I was thinking that what we'll do is celebrate Madeline's third birthday a little earlier, and have a party here with the family. I'll write and let Verity know a date after that. I hope the girls and the children will be able to join us. With this war I know how hard it is to make arrangements to suit us all.' Her tawny eyes suddenly danced. 'But if they can't, at least we had a wonderful Christmas together last year with our usual mix of Hanukkah and Christmas celebrations? Madeline loved lighting the candles on the Menorah and decorating our little Christmas tree, didn't you sweetheart?'

I nodded. 'The lights are pretty,' I said, smiling.

'I'm sure the girls will do their best to be here, Faith, and it will give me time to save the ingredients for her cake,' said Ruth, her spirits lifting at the thought. 'We can play all the games Madeline that your mummy loved for her birthdays, hunt the thimble, pinning the tail on the donkey and dad can draw his wonky donkey! Remember them Faith?' she said with a puckish grin at Owen.

'Thanks for the vote of confidence,' he said, and pulled one of his funny faces at me and I giggled.

'I can tinkle the ivories for pass the parcel,' said Ruth. 'It was always the favourite game with you children. It will be something for us to look forward to and take our minds off this everlasting war.'

Faith got up from her chair and gave Ruth a consoling kiss.

'I do understand how you feel, mum, about us leaving. This damn war! It messes up everybody's lives.' She took my hand. 'Time for bed, Madeline. Where's your *Mabel Lucie Attwell* book?'

'By my bed.'

'She does so love her stories especially the ones of the fairies and elves, the Boo Boos,' smiled Faith. 'Up we go then. Say, Night Night to Granny and Granddad.'

Chapter Three

THE SEA! I could hardly believe my eyes. I stared out of the window at the sea right beside us with a castle rising from the waves as the train drew into Marazion station. I turned to Faith in wonderment. 'It's like the fairy castle in my book,' I exclaimed.

She smiled at my surprise and whilst the train idled for passengers to alight, said, 'That's St. Michael's Mount. It's a magical island Maddy with many legends of mysterious things that have happened there. One of them is about a very bad giant called Cormoran who lived in that castle and he would steal the cattle and sheep from the farmers in Penzance. So the people living on the island decided they had to do something to stop him because he was causing lot of trouble. One night, a boy called Jack, dug an enormous pit at the bottom of the hillside whilst the giant slept. In the morning he crept into the giant's bedroom and blew an ear splitting blast on his horn! The giant was so angry at being woken up that he chased Jack down from the castle and fell straight into the pit and that was the end of him!'

'Were they happy with the giant gone?'

'Yes, they were because now everyone could live in peace. The island was also once a holy place where monks lived, and it is said that the great archangel St. Michael appeared on a rocky ledge to protect the fishermen from treacherous rocks whilst they were out fishing.'

'Did the angel have wings?'

'I don't know. I suppose so,' Faith replied.

'Mrs. Jones didn't.'

Faith looked at me with a puzzled frown. 'You mean Mrs. Jones who lived near Granny and Granddad? The lady we used to see walking her little dog?'

'Yes. She was pretty colours like a rainbow. You said when people die they are angels. Angels *always* have wings. She didn't. Why?'

Faith considered me for a moment. 'Well, if Mrs. Jones had no wings, you must have seen someone else in a pretty coloured dress.'

'No, I *didn't*! I saw Mrs Jones. That lady said Mrs Jones and her bath blew into the garden.'

Faith swallowed in astonishment. 'You remember her saying that?'

'Yes. So she must be an angel. Why didn't she have wings?' I asked again, mulishly.

'Madeline, I can't answer that question because I simply don't know!' Faith replied, her voice impatient at my persistence, and her look was one of relief when the train began to pull away from the station. Within a few minutes it was lurching and slowing down into the terminus at Penzance and before I had a chance to say any more, she quickly stood up and dropping the window on the strap, told me to look out for Verity.

She was waiting on the platform, her eyes searching the carriages as the train came to a screeching halt at the end of the Great Western Line. She was dressed in a belted camel coat, a brown felt hat and muffled up with a knitted woollen scarf against a cold wind. On seeing us, her smile reached out to me from the clouds of steam from the train. I raced to her. She dropped to her knees, and held me tightly to her before standing to embrace Faith, saying how good it was to see us both again and how much I had grown. Her cottage was within walking distance, she said. Picking up one of our suitcases and stepping out from the station we were met with a blast of salty air that sucked my breath away. I skipped between them in high excitement as we walked around the harbour, passing an outdoor sea-water bathing pool and out along the promenade with the same tang of the sea that I remembered when on the ship. To my amazement soap bubbles of white flew around me and laughing at my surprise, Verity said it was sea spray whipped up by the wind.

In no time we were stepping down her garden path and into a small entrance lobby of the cottage where she took our coats and hung them on the pegs. She opened the door into her living room and I sensed the quiet, loving spirit of Verity within its old stone walls and beams. The atmosphere was warm and inviting with comfortable chintz-covered armchairs around a granite fireplace where a log fire flickered above a slate hearth. To each side of the fireplace were alcoves with shelves crammed with books and oriental ornaments of black and red lacquer ware and the intricate designs of two cloisonné vases and a small ivory figurine. A wireless stood on a round occasional table beside one of the chairs and along one wall was an upright piano at which Faith gave a start of pleasure.

'Oh! Verity. A piano!' exclaimed Faith, running the back of her fingers lightly along the keys. 'Last Christmas and at Madeline's birthday party with the family, we had some great singsongs around our old piano. It was like old times.'

Verity gave her a quick hug. 'You can play it as often as you like. I'm afraid I'm not a very accomplished player. Maurice is the pianist. He has a wonderful touch.'

My attention was drawn to a small writing bureau that shone with the patina of years upon which was a photograph of an unsmiling man and woman. I went over and stood looking up at them. The woman sat in a long black dress, corseted tightly to her waist, her face framed with a high lace collar and cameo brooch, and he, standing in a uniform behind her, stared steadfastly at the camera. Verity seeing my interest in the photograph told me they were her parents. The grief at her mother's death formed in pools of tears and I felt guilty for bringing such sorrow to her eyes.

Stairs led us directly up from the living room to a bedroom where one bed stood in a recess beneath a part-sloping ceiling and the other facing the window over-looking the sea.

'This is your bedroom Madeline which you will share with mummy. I've put you in the bed opposite the window so that you can watch the sea. We had to partition off part of the room to create space for a small bathroom,' she said to Faith, 'hence this oddly shaped room. Maurice and I really couldn't face the idea of tin baths in front of the range as you can imagine.'

'You've made it so comfortable for us,' Faith said, noting the bedside lamps and a small book case of paperbacks.

'I remembered you said you like to read before going to sleep, and talking of reading Madeline,' Verity took my hand and led me to the small bedside cupboard beside my bed where a book lay on top. 'Mummy told me you love your *Mabel Lucie Attwell* book and I've managed to find a new one in the bookshop.'

I beamed with pleasure, and looking up I thanked her and was relieved to see her tears had gone. I picked up the book and opened it. 'The pages smell lovely,' I said, sniffing them, and they both laughed.

'Thank you Verity. It was a very kind thought,' said Faith touching her arm affectionately. She moved to the window and gazed out at the choppy sea whipped to white flutes with the wind.

'How wonderful to have this view every day.'

'Yes, I feel very lucky that Maurice and I found this cottage when we did. We've had some very happy holidays here. Something you will enjoy Faith is the fresh fish,' she said with a smile. 'Nothing tastes as good as fish straight out of the sea, when we can get it. It's very restricted because the trawlers are unable to fish by night, and even by day it's hazardous for inshore fishing with the coastline mined as it is. Still, there's always 'toe rag.'

'Toe rag! What on earth is that?' asked Faith.'

'Believe it or not, it's dried salted cod from Iceland, which looks quite revolting. It has to be soaked overnight, then poached the next day and served with a white sauce which the locals call dippy.'

'I can see I will have to familiarize myself with the Cornish lingo!'

'It does take time to get your ear attuned to the dialect and some of the words and sayings are a mystery, but when explained have a canny wisdom and logic to them. The Cornish take time to accept strangers, but once they do, you won't find more loyal friends. Their hospitality is legendary. Over the years, Maurice and I have been pressed to eat their wonderful pasties and saffron cake, and their splits with home made jam and clotted cream—

'Splits?'

'Soft white rolls to you and me. Of course, with rationing, their generosity has been curtailed, and talking of food, you must be hungry. Tea is ready. I made a stew that would keep, in case your train was delayed which it often is these days, so your coming in late was not unexpected.'

'Yes, we were held up for an hour in Plymouth station because of an air raid. It was a bit hairy waiting but here we are, safe and sound.'

'The stew will warm you up after your long journey, Madeline, and stick to those little ribs of yours,' she smiled, gently poking me.

She led us back down the stairs, through the living room and down two stone steps into the kitchen where a small pine table was set for our meal. The room was filled with the savoury smell of cooking, and it glowed warm from the range that glinted with well polished brass handles and fitments.

On sitting down at the table, Faith exhaled a sigh of pleasure, a happy captive to the rustic charm of exposed beams, nooks and crannies and the sea outside the door.

'Your cottage is simply lovely, Verity,' she exclaimed, gazing at the open shelves with Cornish blue and white crockery and oak cupboards beneath the work top. 'It welcomes you in and wraps itself around you.

'Thank you. I'm glad you like it. Maurice and I have put a lot of work into making it a comfortable home for us on our leaves from Malaya.'

'Is it very old Verity?'

'It's one of the earliest houses built along the front but it's still not as old as the Tolcarne Inn which is a pub in Newlyn built in the eighteen hundreds. Maurice enjoys a pint there when we're home.'

Verity began dishing up the stew and all talk of war was kept at bay. Their voices passed to and fro across the table in recollections and light hearted talk of films they had seen and books they had read. There was laughter when Faith recounted a tale of a young trainee nurse swaying up the ward with bedpans piled precariously high in her arms in preparation for the patients' laxatives. 'She was absolutely pickled,' said Faith. 'Someone had laced her drink with gin at a party, and there were frantic efforts to sober her up before Sister's rounds on night shift.'

Soon I began to feel sleepy for it had been a long day on the train and Faith on seeing my eyes closing, lifted me off the chair and carried me up the stairs. I snuggled into her, happy that we three were together again.

From my bed opposite the window the sea and sky was like an ever moving kaleidoscope of colour. In Malaya the sky was hidden by rubber trees and in the evenings, darkness dropped like a stone. Here, I could lie and watch the billowing clouds changing shape into animals and funny faces, marvel at the peach and pink sunsets drifting like one of Faith's chiffon scarves across the skies, see the formation of other worlds of purple mountains, and pistachio coloured lakes, red deserts and flat seas, until with the final rays of the setting sun fringing the clouds, the sky gradually turned to smoky amethyst and became black with stars glinting out over the sea and were hastily shut out of my room with thick black-out curtains.

I soon discovered Cornwall had many moods. There were days of blue skies and cotton wool clouds and others when the sky glowered dark and gloomy with a thick mist that hid the minesweepers in the bay. Out of nowhere, the sea would turn wild and stormy, throwing itself against the sea wall. It became a game I played waiting for the next wave, giggling as it disintegrated over the promenade and drenching unwary walkers, who moved smartly away looking a little foolish. At other times, it was smooth as glass with stars dancing on the water, or was whipped to fluffy white with a sly crafty wind that nipped at my face and legs. Slowly, I found I could not remember Malaya's hot sun pouring down on my skin, the bright red of the hibiscus flowers, the long mornings waiting for daddy to come home for lunch. I tried to remember his face, but I had forgotten it.

'Where's the photo album?' I asked Faith at breakfast.

'It's upstairs in the cupboard by my bed. What's made you think of that so early in the morning?'

'I want to see photographs of daddy. Is he coming home soon?' I asked.

She exhaled sharply. 'No, he's not. How many more times do I have to tell you that?' she snapped.

'You never like me asking about daddy!' I shouted back at her.

Verity looked across the table in surprise at us both.

'There's a war out in Malaya too, Madeline. It's the reason why daddy can't come home yet,' Verity gently explained.

'No it's not! She doesn't love daddy any more, *that's* why I can't see him!' I lashed out.

Faith's eyes widened in disbelief at my outburst, the contours of her face were hard with anger.

'That's *enough* Madeline,' she said fiercely. 'When you've finished your breakfast just *go* upstairs, find the photo album and look at it on your bed.'

I blinked back the tears, smarting at her ferocity and slid from my chair, leaving my cereal half-eaten. I raced upstairs, my breath in ragged wounded gulps, and pulling the album out from the cupboard flung myself on my bed and fighting back tears, began to flip the pages, looking quickly through the black and white snaps browning with age with the corners bent and holding pictures of Granny and Granddad and people I didn't know. I continued flipping the pages until I came to the ones of daddy. I remembered him now. He was tall with dark hair and brown eyes and a scar on his chin. He was pulling me through the water of the swimming pool at the club house in Malaya and there was another of him holding me as we watched the satay man cooking chicken on skewers over a small fire. I

31

suddenly became aware of Faith and Verity's raised voices from downstairs.

'You should be thinking about how this affair will affect Madeline. You're playing with fire, Faith,' I heard Verity say.

It was the first time I'd heard her voice raised in anger and it sent a stab of apprehension through me.

'I don't need your advice, Verity. If you hadn't insisted on knowing why I was so angry with Madeline, you would never have known anything about James. It isn't anybody's business but mine.'

Their quarrelling frightened me and I held Rosie, my dolly close to me and jumping off the bed I went and sat on the window seat.

'I hate this war! It makes everyone angry and unhappy,' I whispered to her. I looked over towards the outdoor swimming pool protected by sand bags and where a gun emplacement stood. No-one was allowed in the pool any more. We had come to Penzance to be safe, but it seemed there was danger here too. I could not play on the beaches as barbed wire covered it from Newlyn to Marazion and mines were laid in the sand and out to sea. I remembered the noise of the bombs dropping on Newlyn damaging eighty homes and Faith saying that mercifully nobody was killed and we were frightened at the raid over the town destroying the centre with incendiary bombs that left the streets with the smell of burning for days and days. I gazed longingly at the magical island and wished and wished that the war would stop so that I could visit it and I could see daddy again.

I stayed upstairs until I dared to come down and was met with a frosty atmosphere in the cottage. In the living room Verity's face was set and venting her anger on the Ewbank, pushing it to and fro with a vengeance and on my retreating from there into the kitchen, I found Faith with the iron and banging the life out of a pile of ironing. The tension between them was everywhere as they skirted one another with forced politeness and spoke only half-heartedly to me. I was under their feet with no escape for outside it was raining, and fetching my box of farm yard animals I retreated back up the stairs to play with them in my bedroom. The album lay on my bed where I had left it. It had caused nothing but trouble. I picked it up and threw it in the cupboard.

'You're very quiet Madeline. What's the matter?' Faith asked when we were eating our dinner in an uneasy silence.

'I heard you upstairs this morning. I didn't mean to make you and Aunt Verity angry about the photo album. Please be friends again,' I pleaded and could feel my eyes swimming with tears.

They stared at me in dismay. Faith jumped up and came to my chair, lifting me up and seating me on her lap.

'There's no need to cry sweetheart, Verity and I had a disagreement about something that's all. It was nothing to do with you or the album.'

'Mummy's right. Sometimes Madeline, grown-ups say silly things to each other and fall out but we'll always be friends. We didn't realize you could hear us. I'm sorry we've upset you.'

In a flurry of guilt, Faith agreed, hunting her hankie out from her apron pocket. 'Now, come on, no more crying. Aunt Verity and I don't like to see you unhappy. We'll finish our dinner and after that we'll have a game of Snap. Would you like that?'

I cheered up. 'Yes! I love playing Snap!'

After our meal, the cards went down fast and furiously and with laughter. I counted mine and was triumphant. I'd won! It was then I noticed the tense atmosphere had vanished along with the rain outside. Shafts of sunlight were beginning to pierce through ragged holes in the clouds, and I felt the cottage settle itself back into the loving warmth I sensed when first I stepped into its rooms.

Chapter Four

THIS DAY IS too good to be inside,' declared Verity, looking out of the window one July morning at the sea sparkling like crystal from a sun that shone blindingly in a cloudless sky.

'Let's all go to St. Ives for the day! The washing can wait until tomorrow,' she said with a playful look at me.

'Yippee!' I yelled.

'And it will do you good, Faith. You've been looking tired these past few days.'

'Yes, I must admit I do feel in need of a change of scenery. It's been particularly busy and hot with the sun beating onto the ward windows.'

'I'll make up a few sandwiches and a flask of tea and can you fetch the picnic blanket from under the stairs Madeline?' Verity said.

I was surprised Verity suggested going to Porthminster beach, kept clear of mines and barbed wire for everyone to enjoy, because we knew women and children had once run for their lives from a hail of German aircraft bullets. Some took to the shelter of the wall below the station, or had ducked behind rocks. Others seeing the face of a crew member in the plane's transparent nose as it came in low over the shoreline strafing the sand and water and with nowhere else to go, ran in a blind panic into the beach tents which afforded little if any protection at all. Later, we learnt the plane had bombed the gasometer in St. Ives.

Today we would take a chance she said as German planes over our towns and coast were few and far between now. In a state of excitement, I ran to the under-stairs cupboard with its reinforced sides and top where we took cover when the enemy planes flew overhead. Verity had made it warm and comfortable with cushions and blankets for us to sleep there until the raids were over, and although it was a tight squeeze, I couldn't help thinking it was so much nicer than Granddad's!

Seated opposite me on the train to St. Ives, two well behaved ladies chatted happily together. I eyed them. Who would believe such a picture of innocence hid a mischievous side like the day I came upon them hooting with laughter at the kitchen table. Quite oblivious to my entrance behind them, I stared transfixed at them both. Verity picked up a half-empty bottle that stood between them and squinted at the label like a blind man. She was dishevelled, her pale skin flushed from fermented wine and wisps of hair were escaping from her normally neat chignon.

'This port's so old you could pickle a body in it!' at which they crumpled into giggling hysteria with tears rolling down their cheeks. Verity gaily topped up their glasses until it spilt and overflowed, trickling down the sides to mingle with the vegetables waiting to be prepared for soup.

Faith drunkenly scooped up the dribbles on her glass and licking her fingers took a large slurp. 'You can pickle me in this any time you like,' she giggled, and hiccupped.

Verity pushed back her chair and said carefully, 'M-u-s-t m-a-k-e t-h-e s-o-u-p.' Swaying to her feet and rooting around in the table drawer, she pulled out a razor sharp chef's knife and began chopping the vegetables. I held my breath as she sliced the vegetables.

Insensible to the blade so close to Verity's fingers, Faith's eyes were glassy as she leaned on the table, one hand propping up her face and the other curled around her glass.

'I haven't told you, have I,' she began, 'about the chef at The Sea View hotel the day the German plane came over Porthminster beach?'

She was speaking in the weirdest way, very slowly and deliberately. Her voice rose and fell like the waves of the sea.

'The hotel cook you see, according to Nursh Treshhider, was unpacking the shhhelfish from the van when the German plane came over. He raced for cover, tripped and dropped the lot! The lobsters took to their claws at this heaven sent opportunity to escape the pot and were later found crawling around in the flower beds.'

The effects of the potent wine simmering away in them erupted again and they both dissolved into snorting uncontrollable laughter.

'Oh! My stomach hurts!' Faith gasped, and picking up the tea cloth from the table, hid her face that was puce with mirth and struggled to compose herself. She took a deep breath.

'Well, that evening with the gas supply kaaaput, the pooor old guests were obliged to make-do with a cold dinner. No lobster for them that night. Wasn't that a shame?!' she said with a smirk.

'An awful shame!' Verity sniggered back, and retrieving the knife she had mercifully dropped onto the table, continued to chop the last of the vegetables.

'Who'd want a lobster for dinner anyway when you can have a delicious soup flavoured with port like us,' she said, as she blithely pushed the meagre vegetables into the saucepan and placed it on the hob. She tipped in a heap of salt and pepper before putting the lid on. 'That should do it!'

I shuddered. It was going to taste horrible.

'Oh *Hello* Madeline,' she said, looking at me pie-eyed, having suddenly noticed me standing there. 'Mummy and I….' she said, looking like a guilty child caught in the act. 'Mummy and I are—'

'Having a silly five minutes with a long forgotten bottle of port,' Faith said, failing to suppress bubbles of laughter. She got unsteadily to her feet and grabbed our hands.

'Come on! Let's dance! Let's do the Hokey-Cokey!' she babbled, and like three demented monkeys, we shook our limbs in and out, singing at the top of our voices, and spinning around until we collapsed dizzily onto the chairs and were suddenly aware that the soup pan was boiling over.

'Oh dear,' said Verity, eyeing the spilt mess on the hob. 'We shall have to have lobster instead!' she said, and they grinned at me like two Cheshire cats.

Speechless, I had looked from one to the other. I was at the mad hatter's tea party!

From the station we walked down the steep steps to Porthminster beach and I skipped ahead of them along the road leading down to where it met the fine golden sand. I was beside myself with excitement, and sitting on the sand, tugged off my socks and sandals to feel the wonderful sensation of it warm between my toes as we walked along the beach to find a spot to ourselves. We spread out, pushing our faces to the sun and taking deep breaths of invigorating sea air. Faith lay down supine on her towel, her sunhat shielding her face and before long she had fallen asleep.

'Poor mummy,' said Verity sympathetically. 'We'll let her have a little nap. She's very tired. Shall we make a sandcastle down by the sea? We can dig a moat and fill it with sea water with your bucket.' We ran laughing down to the tide line and time passed quickly as we busied ourselves heaping sand into a mound. I watched Verity pat and shape it with my spade, and wanting to convey a sudden surge of love for her, I reached across and took her hand. It felt gritty from sand and as she held mine, her smile was one of understanding for the silent pact we were making of friendship, and without really knowing how, or why or when, I knew she would always be a part of my life. In contented companionship we continued finishing the castle with turrets made from my bucket and on glancing back up the beach I saw Faith sit up and look around for us. I waved madly to attract her attention, and jumping to her feet she came running to the waters edge.

'My! You two have been busy. What a lovely castle Maddy. Whooph! I need to cool off. It's hot back there. Are you two coming in with me to have a swim? Madeline, you take my hand and Verity the other and we'll pull you through the water.'

We walked gingerly in to meet the waves, shrieking at the stinging cold, and larking around until chilled to the bone a shivering Verity suggested we got dressed and took a walk around the harbour to the 'island' at Porthmeor where we could have our tea on the grass and enjoy the view over the bay. There was nothing worse, she said, than eating sandwiches coated by sand from an unpredictable breeze whipping in from the sea and with rations getting smaller and smaller by the year fillings were uninspiring enough without the added mix of sand.

We walked along the harbour front past small shops and a closed amusement arcade, and up a steep and cobbled winding pathway of higgledy-piggledy houses tumbling down to the sea, and finally through a narrow road of fishermen cottages that led us to the 'island.' Soon we were nestled in the springy turf and with our sandwiches eaten and tea drunk, we lay back and lazily watched the white fringed waves rippling in and out of the bay. Replete from our food and lulled into a state of hypnotic stupor by the warmth of the sun, the sound of the sea and the odd buzz of a bumble bee, Verity startled the life out of us by suddenly leaping to her feet.

'Just look at those gannets, Faith!' she cried. 'They're following the fish across the bay. Look! Madeline, look!' she pointed.

I watched the gannets diving like arrows into the sea, folding their wings a split second before entering into the commotion of water. They were like bombs dropping from the sky, awakening in me the frightening memory of the bomb blast in Granny and Granddad's house.

'What an amazing sight, Verity,' said Faith, sitting down again on the blanket.

'Yes, it is. You don't often see them so close to shore—

'Are Granny and Granddad alright?' I butted in.

'Yes, of course they are.' Faith gave me a doubtful look. 'Are you worried about them because there's no need to be? They're fine.'

'A bomb blast broke Granny's vases, Aunt Verity, and my egg disappeared! And Mrs. Jones died. She's an angel now. I saw her.'

Verity blinked. 'Did you now?!'

'Yes, but she didn't have wings!'

Confused by the minute, Verity's eyes questioned Faith, who shaking her head said,

'Don't even ask!'

'And Mummy was so happy when your letter came asking us to stay with you. She danced with me around the room!'

'What on earth has brought all this on?' Faith asked, grinning self-consciously.

'Well I was very happy that you came,' Verity said, her mouth curving into a smile.

'We came here to be safe from the war, didn't we mummy? But it's all over the place, isn't it? ' I said, flinging my arms wide to encompass the earth and sky.

'We might think we've shielded her from the worst of it but children understand far more about this war than we realize,' I heard Verity murmur to Faith.

She glanced at her watch. 'I think it's time for us to make a move and head back to the station,' she said. 'Madeline, would you like to help me fold up the blanket whilst mummy packs away the picnic things.'

We were waiting on the platform when I saw the twins. They were standing between a man and woman with another little girl beside them in a pushchair. It was their hair that first caught my attention, for it was the same strawberry blond as mine. I peered around Faith to take a closer look and stared in amazement. They were so like me, I was spellbound. They were dressed identically in cotton print dresses with ties to the back and Peter Pan collars and wore white socks and sandals. The one who stood slightly behind the other, smiled back at my stare with eyes that were luminous and green as emeralds. A heightened awareness of recognition ran through me. I tingled all over with it. But how could that be? I had no memory of seeing them before. The twin in front, sensing my interest, gazed back at me and poked out her tongue before turning to the girl in the pushchair, playfully jingling the beads stretched across the base of the hood. I was piqued. How rude but I was curious and strangely drawn to them. I began to edge their way, but Faith caught my hand, for the train was steaming in to a squealing halt at the buffers. We piled into one of the carriages and the twins disappeared from view into the crowd. I stared from my window at glimpses of the turquoise sea and golden sands and in the far distance Godrevy lighthouse, but my mind was gripped with the mystery of the twins as we rounded corners of the picturesque line between St. Ives and St. Erth. There was something at variance about the twin who smiled at me. Unlike her sister, whose movements were like quicksilver, she had a stillness and radiance as if the sun shone from within her. It suddenly struck me. She was shining like Mrs. Jones who died. But this girl could not be dead. She was with her family. It was mystifying. I had to see them again and the very second we came into St. Erth station I craned my neck at the carriage door to see above the crowds.

'Who are you looking for?' Faith asked. 'You're holding everyone up,' giving me a light push for me to jump down onto the platform.

Some instinct within me held my tongue to any detail of them. 'Just two girls I saw at St. Ives,' I answered, carelessly.

We crossed the bridge to wait for our connecting train back to Penzance and it was then I caught sight of them in the press of people across from our platform. They were going in the opposite direction. So that's why I've never seen them before, I thought. They live in another town. When their train came into view, the sunshine twin vanished as if into thin air. I kept looking for her amongst the crowd, but she had gone, and her twin sister and the family seemed not to have noticed her disappearance at all. I couldn't forget the twins and the strange feeling I had of familiarity with them. When we were out I scanned buses and trains and our town, always hoping to see them, and then I started school, and they slipped to the back of my mind like an itch I could not scratch.

***

Less than a year later on a May morning we heard a cacophony of church bells ringing and the blaring of horns from every boat in the bay and harbour. The war was over! It was on everyone's lips. We ran outside and were caught up in an explosion of rejoicing, a jubilant uplifting of spirits. Everyone seemed to be infected with a collective madness. I watched in amazement Verity and Faith embracing their neighbours and strangers who had emerged from the Queen's Hotel further along the promenade. The promenade filled with people laughing and talking and a man with grey hair broke into song, *there'll always be an England* at which they fell silent and listened with tears of joy.

I was accustomed to Faith's emotional responses to situations, but this was a side of Verity that took me by surprise. She was excited as a child. 'I must hang out our flag,' she cried, running back inside.

I followed her up the stairs.

'Oh, how we've waited for this,' she sang, hunting for a large Union Jack at the back of her wardrobe. Giggling together, we ran to my bedroom. She flung open the sash window, unfurling the flag, and waved it gaily around at Faith below, before dropping the window onto the pole and running back downstairs with me to join once again in the celebrations.

There was a sobering moment and sympathy with one of our neighbours who had lost her only son. Verity and Faith hugged her amidst her tears of gladness

43

overshadowed with a sadness for all those like herself who would never see their loved ones again. For her it was a bitter sweet ending and for us only one thought marred our happiness, we had not heard when the war would be ending in the Far East. Despite this nothing could detract from the joy we felt, the euphoria on surviving a war that was finally over.

That night, I knelt up at my bedroom window. The hateful black-out curtains were pulled back, leaving pools of friendly light spilling out onto the garden from our windows and others all along the promenade. Boat lights twinkled around the bay and from the fishing villages of Newlyn and Mousehole. It was the most magical sight I had ever seen. I gazed in wonder at it all, until Verity came in to kiss me goodnight. 'Mummy will be up in a minute.'

She looked happy and relaxed. 'The lights are lovely, aren't they? You will be able to see them every night now.' She drew me back into bed. 'No need for a story tonight I think after such a wonderful day.' She tucked me in and I hugged her tightly to me as she kissed me goodnight.

I lay back against my pillow watching the black swell of the sea flash with white tipped waves. I wanted to stay awake all night listening to the murmuring sea mingling with bursts of war-time songs from our neighbours singing around Faith playing the piano. I struggled against the pull of sleep, waiting for her, and thinking that soon I would at last be able to visit my fairytale castle. I sleepily felt her kiss and the stroke of her fingers through my hair before I drifted away and in the morning when I asked about visiting the castle, I discovered my patience would be tried even longer, for they said it would be some time before the beach could be cleared of mines and barbed wire, enabling us to walk across the causeway to the magic island.

Chapter Five

VERITY COULD NOT settle to any task and finally seated herself with a book in the window. It was impossible. She had read the same paragraph again and again, her mind refusing to make sense of the words in front of her. She gave in and stared at the sea, remembering the day she had met Maurice at the Christmas ball. Tall and distinguished looking with expressive hands, her heart leapt when he asked her to dance. From that first meeting of mutual attraction, they fell deeply in love, and the delightful discovery that it was also a meeting of minds, only added to their happiness. A mixture of excitement and apprehension clutched at her heart at the thought of seeing him again after so many years apart. Would they still have the same depth of feelings for each other? She had seen enforced separation destroying marriages with men returning home to find their wives were no longer content with home and children having tasted independence working in the factories, on farms and in joining the forces. For the first time in their lives they were on an equal footing with the same freedom as men and were forming relationships outside of marriage. Husbands expecting life to continue as before were perplexed to find their wives had become strangers, and those women that had waited discovered life would never be the same again with men damaged by war. She could not believe that a love as strong as theirs would wither from lack of contact, but his letters to her were brief and few and in the end had stopped altogether. The very brevity of his words had gnawed away at her for they were quite unlike his familiar style of writing that spoke of his love of literature with scattered quotations and lines of their shared love of poetry by Bryon, Shelly, and Keats.

It was not until she heard from her friend Deidre, who, on arriving in England, wrote of their terror of the overrunning of Malaya by the Japanese that Verity had the first indication of how alarming the situation was. She said Maurice dropped out of sight some months before the Japanese assault and was fairly certain he had not been rounded up for internment. Rumours abounded of men training and infiltrating behind Japanese lines, but in the chaos and panic, no-one really had any clear idea of what was happening. Deirdre's news offered a small hope and reason for his scant letters. Verity also realized how opportune the timing was of her leaving Malaya. Deidre and little daughter had not been so lucky, having to race to Singapore with the bombs dropping around them, as they scrambled aboard in the crush of women and children, some falling from the quayside with the surge of people towards the companionway onto one of the last boats out of the port. It was a seven week nightmare of a journey home, enduring cramped and stiflingly hot conditions, sleeping with the majority of passengers on mattresses in a large area below deck. In the Sunda straits they were bombed again, suffering a near miss when eating their meals at two long tables. It was terrifying, she wrote, for the reverberation had sent the ship rolling from side to side with crockery and cutlery sliding onto the floor and ending up in a heap between the tables. Despite reading of the horrors her friend and children had endured in their race to get out, Verity put her faith in the thought that Maurice had escaped. He was fluent in Chinese and Malay, a strategic advantage if he had taken to hiding and fighting with the indigenous peoples in the jungles of Malaya. He was not a man for surrender.

With Maurice's imminent arrival, Faith had arranged to pick Madeline up from school and take her to a friend's house where they would stay for a couple of nights. Verity was touched at Faith's thoughtfulness at giving them time alone for those first few precious hours. She looked at her watch. It was time to change into her Sunday dress, a soft print of pale blue, the style a flattering crossover bodice with softly gathered shoulder yokes and a belted midriff. In the mirror, she looked pale, and dabbed powdered rouge onto her cheeks, and a slick of colour with the last stub of her lipstick that she had saved for his homecoming. Already her heart was thumping at the thought of seeing him as she shrugged into a square shouldered jacket. She pinned on her hat, picked up her handbag and gloves, and with one last look at herself in the mirror at her unpinned hair falling smoothly around her face, the way Maurice liked it, she set off walking briskly along the prom.

She stood on the platform, her eyes seeking him, her body trembling with anticipation as the train came into the station. Doors banged open. With a stifled cry she saw him looking anxiously around the crowded platform, and she flew down the platform, her eyes alight, her arms wide to hold him. Dear God, his face was devoid of colour, and he was so thin, she could feel the frailness of him through his coat.

'Oh darling, it's been so long. I can't believe you're here.' She had resolved not to cry, to be the smiling Verity at the dockside when seeing her off, but her will deserted her. 'I'm being such a ninny,' she said, pushing her tears away, 'but it's so so good to have you home.'

They clung to one another, a world of waiting in his touch, his eyes searching her face to assure himself she was not a mirage.

'Verity, Verity, my wonderful girl,' he murmured.

She had been warned by the civil service that he was not well, and had ordered a taxi, but the weakness in his step alarmed her. She held his arm, guiding him into the seat. He sat back, closing his eyes, and holding tightly her hand, sighed. 'Home at last.'

***

I was half-asleep when I heard a cry like the pain of a wounded animal.

'No! Not James! He can't be.'

With a beating heart, I slipped from the sheets and crept to the half-open door.

'I'm sorry to have been the one bringing you such upsetting news, Faith,' I heard Maurice say. 'I have a letter for you from him. It was written some time before his death. He asked me to give it to you if anything happened to him.'

'A letter? Dear God. It's as if he knew he wasn't going to make it.'

Verity sounded strained. 'This is what Faith feared Maurice when she hadn't heard from James.'

'I don't mean to sound harsh,' said Maurice, 'especially now when you're so upset but maybe, when you've had time to accept it, this could be a chance to make a fresh start with Roger.'

'But you don't understand. You don't understand at all. How could you?' Faith cried out.

'Madeline is *James's* child! We were making plans to start a new life together with her. I could never go back

to Roger. Never! He's nothing but a philandering bastard,' she said bitterly.

There was a long silence and then I heard Faith's voice at the foot of the stairs, husky with tears and emotion.

'I think I'll have an early night. I'm exhausted. Thank you Maurice for giving me James's letter and I'm sorry to have put such a damper on your homecoming. I will explain everything tomorrow, when I'm more myself. I'm so glad you're safely home. Verity has loved and missed you more than she would ever admit.'

I ran to my bed and feigned sleep. I heard her coming up the stairs, the water running in the bathroom, her footsteps into our room. I lay with my heart in my mouth from fear. I had never known Faith to cry. She was like sunshine to me, her smile lighting up her eyes from a tangle of bouncing hair around her face. She was as vital and richly colourful as a butterfly in her long bright summer skirts and scarves, padding barefooted around our bedroom and calling for me to brush and tame her hair by tying it back with an Indian silk scarf, fine as gossamer. She made us laugh no matter how tired after her shift, conjuring up amusing tales of hospital life and bringing happiness into our cottage.

I heard the rustle of clothes discarded and the creak of the bed as she slipped between the sheets. Through half-closed eyes I watched her read the letter. Her tears fell like rain.

'Oh James, James,' she whispered, holding the letter to her.

I was an interloper on her sadness, wishing the tall thin man had never come to our house with a letter that made her so unhappy. Again and again she read it, her body wracked with misery, until she finally placed it beneath her pillow. She switched off her bedside light and the blackness of night enveloped us both leaving only the sigh of the waves washing to and fro over the pebbles to quell my fears and lull me to sleep.

With Faith still working in the hospital, Verity continued to take and bring me home from school, but I missed her undivided attention. Faith explained she needed to look after Maurice until he got better from his illness of dysentery and malaria from his years fighting in the jungle which left him with recurring bouts of fever and chills and debilitating muscle pain. Faith also kept a close eye on him, but from me she had withdrawn into a world of her own. Her eyes that once danced with life were now as dark as a tin mine and filled with tears.

'Aunt Verity, why is mummy always crying? Have I done something wrong?' I asked.

'Of course not,' she said, hugging me to her. There was annoyance at my mother beneath her calm façade, nor was I fooled when she brightly suggested we took a walk along the prom to the semi-tropical Morrab gardens to watch the goldfish. My resentment grew with each step. This man had slipped into our circle of three like a thief in the night and stolen our happiness.

And then, one hot summer's day I saw Faith's hollow, distant look had vanished. Her sunshine was back.

'Hello, sweetheart,' she said, as I came out to her. She looked up at me with a happy smile from weeding the flower bed edging the path to the front door where it framed the ordered rows of carrot tops, potatoes, lettuces, tomato and runner beans.

'Uncle Maurice said to tell you, he's going to take me for a jaunt along the prom because he fancies a pint with Mr. Uren who lives in a cottage opposite the Tolcarne Inn. He's hoping Mrs. Uren will be pleased to have a horrible pink shrimp like me for company whilst they're in the pub.'

'Oh, I *see*! Leaving us workers to it,' she teased, pushing away with the back of her earth-stained hand rebellious tendrils of hair escaping her bandeau. She glanced at my sun burnt arms and legs.

'Uncle Maurice is right. You have caught the sun. I'll put on some Calamine lotion before you go to bed tonight.'

Maurice appeared. 'See you later. We're off to an undercover rendezvous, aren't we Madeline?'

'You are, are you,' laughed Faith, playing along. 'Can I join you?'

'Only those who know the secret pass word are allowed to come!'

'Oh! So it's like that is it? I shall have to make do with a kiss, instead.'

I bent to kiss her cheek, and she caught and held me close. 'I know I've been a grumpy old mum, lately. Will you forgive me?'

I nodded and beamed at her, and on an impulse, turned a summersault on the path with the sheer joy of seeing Faith in such good spirits.

They both laughed at my display.

'Well...Toodel-oo!' sang out Maurice taking my hand.

I looked back at Faith and waved, bursting with happiness as we walked along the prom with the now redundant gun emplacement and the thriving allotments on the dug-up bowling green. I noticed for the first time Maurice was walking with a spring in his step as he related to me his encounters with the snakes and animals and the big beautiful butterflies in the jungles of Malaya. His face once lined and thin had plumped out and sported a neat moustache. My antagonism at his intrusion into our lives began to melt away. I decided I liked him. He was really rather nice and he made me laugh.

'So, how did you enjoy your walk and a pint?' Verity asked, looking up from her magazine on our return. 'Faith's in the kitchen making us a cup of coffee. We haven't long come inside.'

Faith appeared carrying a tray with the coffee cups.

'We enjoyed ourselves very much, didn't we Madeline?'

'Oh yes, Mrs. Uren gave me a slice of cake and a drink and she showed me the dinkiest ornaments of little animals and houses. Look, she gave me one of a little black and white cat.' I carefully extracted it from tissue paper in my dress pocket. 'Can I put it on the cupboard beside my bed?'

'Yes, of course you can, sweetheart. How kind of her,' said Faith. 'I hope you remembered to thank her.'

'M-u-m-m-y! You know I would!'

'The pub is just as I remembered it,' Maurice said, 'dark and smoky from the old boys jawing by the fire with their pipes. They still serve a cracking pint of beer. I used to dream about it during the war. A few of the locals came in for an early pint, and we chatted about the history of the characters that have lived and worked in Newlyn. I was sorry to hear their barman copped it at Dunkirk. Nice young lad.'

'Oh I am sorry to hear that too,' replied Verity. 'I liked him. He always had a ready smile for the customers.'

Faith glanced at the clock on the mantelpiece and back at me. 'I'll make your cup of cocoa, and put some Calamine lotion on your arms and legs, and then it's time for bed.'

'Oh, do I have to? Couldn't I stay up a little bit longer, mummy? It's still daylight. I'll be ever so good,' I said with an ingratiating grin.

'Nothing doing my girl,' she replied, 'it's cocoa and bed!'

I looked in vain at Verity for support. 'You'll fall asleep in no time after your walk in the fresh air,' she said, amused at my wheedling.

'But I don't feel a bit tired,' I said, on Faith's return with the drink and a bottle of Calamine.

'Tired or not, young lady, you're going up those stairs! Now, drink up.'

Later, she came and sat on the edge of my bed beside me. I put down my *Enid Blyton* book.

'You enjoyed your jaunt with Uncle Maurice, then?'

'Yes, I like Uncle Maurice, now. I didn't at first,' I ventured, 'because he made you cry.'

Faith looked at me askance. 'What are you talking about?'

'He gave you a letter, didn't he? And you cried and put it under your pillow.'

Faith was discomfited. 'You shouldn't have been watching me. It was private.'

I squirmed. 'Who's James, mummy?'

Her eyes widened. 'Oh, just someone I knew in Malaya. A friend,' she replied, forestalling any further questions by looking away out to sea. 'There's a fishing boat returning with his catch,' she said, changing the subject. 'Tomorrow, we'll see if we can buy some fish from the quayside at Newlyn for our dinner.' She turned back and kissed me goodnight, smoothing my forehead and studying my face with a look of tenderness, as if recalling a memory.

She rose. 'You can read for a little while longer, if you like, until it gets dark.' She gave a soft sigh and for a fleeting moment, I saw her eyes were twin mirrors of sadness.

53

***

I was scratching away with my nail at Jack Frost on my window pane when I caught sight of the postman walking gingerly along the snowy pavement. My hopes soared for a special letter or postcard for me from Granny and Granddad, which they had sent on a regular basis throughout the war. He was leaning over to open our gate with a letter in his hand. Yippee! Another one for me to stick in my special scrapbook of Granddad's stories with funny sketches drawn in the margins. I raced down the stairs and waited for it to drop onto the mat and groaned with disappointment. It was for Faith and feeling disheartened I took it to her.

'It's from Roger! It's been redirected by mum and dad,' said Faith, ripping it open at the kitchen table amidst the remains of breakfast. She quickly scanned the page. 'Well, this is a turn-up for the books. He writes he's filled with remorse for his behaviour. Feeling sorry for himself more like,' Faith said with a cynical look at Verity. 'He's hoping for a reconciliation and says he's misses Madeline.'

My heart leapt. 'Does the letter mean daddy's coming home now?' I asked warily, remembering her anger the last time I had asked this.

She frowned. 'I don't know. Have you done your spelling homework?' The subject was closed.

'Yes, I've done my spelling. It was easy-peasy.' I changed tack. 'Where's Uncle Maurice?'

'He's gone to fetch a newspaper. Look, why don't you go into the living room and read your new library book? The fire is lit.'

With a large pointed huff of protest, I submitted and stamped my feet up the steps into the living room. I knelt on the window seat, and saw to my delight the snow was beginning to fall again covering the sound of the odd car along the prom, the chatter of people walking by, and the harsh bark of a dog being taken for a run along the sea front. Even the rhythmic swish of the sea's ebb and flow seemed to bow to the beauty and silence of the snow and was muted, and from the kitchen I could hear the clear cadence of their voices and the clatter of domesticity.

'It's rather late in the day to say he's sorry and I have no wish for a reconciliation. James may have died but I still love him and always will. I thank God I still have a part of him in Madeline.'

A chair was scraped back from the table with the clicks of breakfast dishes being cleared.

'From what you say Roger's written, it sounds like he had similar experiences to James and Maurice except he was eventually caught and interned. The stories and pictures now coming out of these camps are horrifying. Heaven only knows what he's suffered.'

'I know and despite everything I hate to think of Roger suffering in such a barbaric way. He hasn't said very much about it other than he had to go into hospital for while after the closing of the camp because he was in a bit of a mess. It's obvious he's playing down what happened to him out there. After his discharge from hospital he reported to reception depots for medical reports and personal details to be recorded before repatriation. He was thinking of returning home but decided in view of our separation, to stay behind and get back to work on bringing the estate up to scratch.'

'Have you thought about giving him another chance? The sort of experience he's had can alter people, makes them realize what a mess they've made of their lives. This war has changed everyone's way of life; people losing wives, husbands, sons and daughters. It puts a different perspective on things, on his too, by the sound of it, and you must have loved him once?'

'Yes, I did. He swept me off my feet, but I soon learnt the old saying, marry in haste and repent at leisure. I can't even say I wasn't warned by the nurses. They told me men from abroad hung around the teaching hospitals looking for a wife on their home leaves. With only a few months to find one, they have to move quickly and he certainly did that. If I did return to him I still don't feel he has the right to know anything about my affair with James, and certainly not about Madeline after the way he treated me.'

'You take a risk by not telling him. Anyone can see Madeline looks nothing like Roger and these things often have a way of coming out of the closet. And then there's Madeline herself. If she should discover the truth, it will be a tremendous shock. Promise me you will tell her when she's old enough to understand.'

'I'll cross that bridge when I come to it.'

'Well, I hope so. Whatever you decide to do, either way, Roger should know the truth about Madeline. Maurice agrees with me. He's a stickler for good form, and feels it would be the only decent thing to do. By wiping the slate clean if you should rejoin him, you can both make a fresh start.'

The dishes clattered around in the enamel washing-up bowl.

'That's easy for you two to say. What respect or loyalty did he ever give to me, associating with women behind my back?

Look, I did my best to make this marriage work. I didn't expect soon after my arrival to have the shock and humiliation of overhearing in the club's powder room a woman saying my husband was a womaniser and far worse, had fathered a child to Janita our Tamil amah. I felt sick to the pit of my stomach, and demanded to know the truth from him. He vehemently denied it and yet from the minute she came into our house I instinctively felt ill at ease with her although she was respectful enough to my face and I saw no sign of a child. Despite all that, I was determined to prove those women wrong and Roger seemed pleased that I dismissed their talk as malicious gossip. But as the months went by I began to see women were the oxygen of his life. He could no more resist a pretty face than a humming bird could the nectar. His excuses for his absence I believed for a while until my eyes were finally opened when watching him with a newcomer to the club. He was gazing down at her with the full Johnson offensive and dancing so shamelessly close to her I was hurt and embarrassed beyond endurance. On return home I pleaded for him to stop his humiliating behaviour and he denied he had done anything wrong, and said it was all in my mind. I couldn't believe his pathetic attempt to turn the tables on me and it turned into a blazing row with him slamming out of the house and me screaming after him. It was just awful. I felt drained and more than anything else angry that he was turning me into a suspicious screaming harridan. When I calmed down I wondered why he married me, he was sitting pretty with an amah on tap. What a naïve little fool I was.'

'He probably felt the need to settle down with a wife and family and you shouldn't be so hard on yourself. Roger was considerably older and knew his way around and you had little experience of men from which to judge him.'

'Yes, that's true and I do believe in his own skewed way he loved me, probably still does, but he has this fatal flaw in his make-up and like a leopard is never going to change his spots. It didn't take him long to discover a wife hindered his freedom. And look how it ended up, me having a baby with another woman's husband.'

'You were vulnerable. I've no doubt if Roger hadn't played around, it would never have happened. You have a lot to weigh up, now. Take your time. Think of what's best for Madeline. She needs a father. And I wish you'd felt you could have shared this with me before. It makes it more understandable you're reluctance to make a fresh start with Roger.

'Yes, I should have done and I'm sorry for that. It was just that I wanted to put the whole messy business of Roger behind me and after the war start a new life with James.'

'All I know is during the years I lived in KL I saw a lot of silly behaviour from men and women, but there was an unwritten rule whites did not consort with the locals,' Verity replied. 'Of course we knew a blind eye was turned when men were suddenly out of town on so called business trips, seeking comfort in the 'kip' shops, and some on lonely outstations took up with their housekeepers, or 'keeps' as they were known, until the memsahib turned up from home. Marriages can and do survive it.'

'I'm sure they do. As you say, I've a lot to think about before I decide what to do. Oh and since when has sex been called comfort?!' and I heard them chuckling.

***

The wonderland of snow had gone, and the rain was beating on the windows in heavy gusts from the wind. I sat in the kitchen in a bubble of contentment after school, cocooned in the warmth of the range, and tranquillized with the ticking of the clock. The savoury smell of a pie cooking edged around my nose. From the living room I could hear the fire being riddled, the scrape of the shovel into the coal scuttle. I concentrated on painting the last bit of the lady's dress in my colouring-in book. It was done. I slipped from the chair and came up from the kitchen into the living room to show them my picture.'

'Meanwhile, it's time Madeline and I returned to London,' Faith was saying, looking pink from the heat as she knelt back on her heels from the grate.

I felt a flicker of alarm go through me.

'I've imposed on you and Maurice long enough since his return, and my parents have been wondering when I shall be bringing Madeline to see them before we return to Malaya,' she said, getting up from the fireplace. She gave Verity an affectionate touch on her shoulder as she passed her chair and sat down opposite on the other side of the fire.

'I've such a lot to thank you for Verity. You've been a wonderful friend to me and I know I couldn't have survived this war without you. I shall miss you so much.'

Verity smiled. 'Friendship works both ways,' she replied, her hands busy knitting a pullover for Maurice. 'You'll never know how glad I was when you took up my invitation to stay with me. Life would have been pretty miserable without you and Madeline throughout this war. We've faced the ups and downs and hardships together and it goes without saying how much I shall miss you too and it's going to seem very strange not having a little girl around any more,' she said, with a regretful look at me.

'Well I know Maddy has loved every minute of living by the sea with you. You two have become as thick as thieves!'

Verity laughed. 'I think the world of her.'

I beamed my love back.

'I've been thinking over everything you and Maurice have advised about the situation with Roger,' Faith went on, 'And I've decided that coming so soon after his internment it would not be the best time to tell him anything about James or Madeline. And I need time to sort out my own feelings and see how things work out once we're together again. It's not going to be easy.'

'No, I'm sure it won't be but I still think you're doing the right thing to give him another chance, if nothing else, for Madeline's sake.'

Tired of the talk and waiting to show her my picture, I thrust it in front of Faith's face.

'That's lovely,' Faith said automatically, irritated I had interrupted their conversation, but my attention had suddenly focused with a sinking feeling on her remark that we would be leaving for London.

'I don't want to leave here, mummy. Please say we can stay with Aunt Verity,' I begged.

'We have to return to Malaya sometime, Maddy,' Faith replied. 'You've asked enough times about your father, haven't you? Well, now the war's over, you will be able to see him. Won't that be lovely?' she said brightly.

'But I—'

'Not only that, you've been saying you wanted to see Granny and Granddad, again. Well, now you will. We shall stay with them for a while before leaving for Malaya. Why don't you paint another picture? You could give it to Verity. I'm sure she will love to have a reminder of you and will find a space in her drawer to keep it after we've gone.'

'I shall do better than that. I shall have it framed Madeline and hang it in my bedroom where I can see it every night before I go to sleep.'

I glowed with pleasure and going to her chair, bent to kiss her. She took my face in her hands, her eyes loving, and attempting to make light of our parting, she said, 'I don't know what Maurice is going to do without his undercover partner on his medicinal walks.'

I smiled sadly. 'And do you think Mrs. Uren will miss me and our little talks?'

'I'm quite sure she will. Now off you go and paint me that picture,' she laughed, giving my bottom a light tap on the way.

I fetched some clean water for the jam jar and sitting at the kitchen table I carefully dipped and stroked colour between the lines of a cottage with flowers in the garden, wanting it to be the best picture I'd ever painted to give to Aunt Verity. Faith and Aunt Verity were always talking about her friend James, I thought, as the colours filled the page, and it also dawned on me that grown-ups lied just as children did. No matter how hard she tried to hide it, Faith did not really want to see daddy again. She was returning to Malaya because of me.

Chapter Six

Cornwall 1963

I TURNED THE key and stepped into Verity's cottage with a sigh of relief that my shift on the children's ward was over. It had been a particularly busy and demanding day. One little girl admitted with meningitis and a boy with pneumonia. It would be touch and go as to whether she would pull through but the boy had a good chance of full recovery. There had been the usual spate of broken limbs with the school summer holidays in full swing, a toddler with severe burns, having pulled a pan of boiling water over himself and brought in by ambulance with his frantic mother, to be shortly followed by an equally distraught father, whose son had been crushed under their farm tractor. The father was as pale as his son and said shakily his boy was lucky not to have been killed. Even so, his injuries to his legs and pelvis required immediate surgery. His summer helping his father on the farm was over for his body would take months to heal.

Verity's cottage had been our haven from the laying waste of war, and once again had become mine following the end of a turbulent love affair. Faith and I were desperately upset when Verity wrote to say the jungle warfare and the illness arising from it had affected Maurice's health in later years and he'd had a massive stroke and died suddenly. Although I had seen him only infrequently in the intervening years, he remained a special memory, a man whose piano playing inspired a love of classical music, who never talked down to me, and was a source of information and hilarity on our undercover walks. I had loved them both and felt such an overriding sadness for Verity left alone with no friends or family any longer in Surrey and understood why she had decided to remain in Malaysia, a city she loved for its colourful polyglot of nationalities, a city which was modernising and expanding by the year, where life could pass pleasantly with her many friends playing mahjong and bridge, and continue with her love of Japanese painting and Ikebana. Soon she would be back in Cornwall for the summer months and I was looking forward to our catching up on our lives, long walks together, and the happiness of just being with her.

I went upstairs, slipping into the freedom of a long loose fitting skirt and top, and looking out of the window on a deceptively benign sea that could be as capricious as the wind, my mind went back to the night of the storm that came raging in from another continent; a tyrant of an ocean hurling itself over the wall and slamming down pebbles and gritty sand along the promenade. The wind its willing accomplice screamed around my window pane, flinging sea-spray that disintegrated with a stinging slap on the glass. In the midst of this tumult, out of no-where, he appeared at the foot of my bed. His fair hair was shot through with the red of a sunset, like mine, and I felt no fear for his grey green eyes shone with love for me, and his smile was deep and comforting. He did not stay long, and to my amazement faded away, yet I sensed he was still there watching over me and all these years I'd wondered who he was and why he came. And as I stood lost in my thoughts of that wild night, and mesmerised by the movement of the dancing sea, the hairs on my arms rose. How could I have been so blind? It stared me in the face and was undeniable. I had his eyes and hair colouring and he looked at me with the love of a father. There was never a need to ask Faith what James looked like. I had seen him with my own eyes and he had shown me that the love and spirit of a man never dies. I skipped down the stairs imbued with a joyous state of being. I went into the kitchen and poured myself a long, cool drink of Cinzano and lemonade and went out into the garden. I flopped into the deckchair, drinking in the sea air and with my head fizzing with memories.

The years after the war drifted around me. Roger, on our arrival in Malaya was thin and haggard from his years of interment, his gaunt eyes looking at Faith and then at me, as if trying to place us in the frame of his life again.

'And is this my darling baby girl? All grown up now. Come and give your daddy a kiss.'

He opened his arms to me but I stayed close to Faith. It was the moment I had longed for and driven Faith to distraction to see but now I was caught unawares. He had become a stranger.

He looked hurt and bewildered.

'She was very young when we left here, Roger. Give her time.'

'And how are you Faith? You look well,' he said, planting an awkward kiss on her cheek.

'Do I? Thank you,' she said, flatly.

He was ill at ease at her lack of response, his eyes darting around the room, and back at us both. 'Uh, we have a new amah. I thought you'd appreciate me finding a Malay one from the kampong. Her name is Aishah. She's young and willing to learn.'

'I see. Well, that's a step in the right direction.'

'As I said on my letter, I'm hoping we can make a fresh start, Faith,' he replied, with a pronounced nervous twitch.

A flicker of pity crossed Faith's face at this outward sign of his cruel ordeal in the concentration camp. 'We'll talk about that later, shall we?' she said. 'I'll take our suitcases into the bedroom and unpack, and perhaps Aishah can make us a glass of fresh orange. It so long since we've had it, I've practically forgotten what an orange looks like!'

The atmosphere for weeks remained a constrained truce. Young as I was, I could see they were fencing around each other, Roger doing all he could to please and Faith putting on a show for my sake. Her nature was one of natural warmth and interaction and she found it hard to remain cold and distant with him.

In time, I sensed the beginning of a change in the air. Roger became a man less haunted by his night terrors and our lives took on the pattern and slow rhythm of life in the tropics. I returned home once a week from Kuala Lumpur where it had been arranged for me to stay with Aunt Verity and Maurice enabling me to attend the newly formed Alice Smith School for there was no education for ex-patriot children in our area. It was a situation I accepted with undisguised delight. With the constant shifting of moods between Faith and Roger as they acclimatised to each other once more, I guiltily felt freer and more relaxed with Aunt Verity and Maurice. I became his undercover partner again on excursions to the Royal Selangor Club, known as The Spotted Dog because, he said, on one of our walks there, a very naughty lady brought her black and white Dalmatian dogs to the club. This was strictly prohibited, and they bounded around knocking glasses off the rattan tables with their tails! One could never be sure with Maurice's tales, and I gave him a disbelieving playful push. 'It's quite true,' he laughed, giving me a push back and I grinned at him. He was always such fun to be with.

On school holidays my friend Jean and I stayed with each other, and Faith took us on trips to the beautiful tree fringed golden sands of the Blue Lagoon on Pankor Island. Other days found us splashing around in the pool at the club, and afterwards, starving hungry, we waited impatiently for the satay man to cook over a wood burner the pieces of chicken on sticks and when ready we dipped them into the delicious spicy peanut sauce, stuffing it down our faces and giggling with the joy of just being alive and together.

Two years later, my routine and settled world crashed down on returning home from school to find Faith packing. Her cheeks were red, her tawny eyes fiery with anger.

'We're leaving,' she snapped. 'We shall stay with Aunt Verity in KL for a few days, and then we're going home to granny and granddad's until I can find a place of our own.'

'But why?' I cried out. 'I don't want to leave here.'

'We are going and that's that!' she answered, yanking open the chest of drawers and piling the contents in a heap on the bed.

'What about Jean? I won't be able to see her any more. 'It's not fair.' I shouted.

Her voice was tight with temper. 'You can shout and scream as much as you like! We are going home!'

'I thought *this* was home? And what about daddy? Is he coming too?'

'No, he's not!' she shrieked at me.

I was crushed at her anger. 'Is it my fault again?' I asked nervously.

Faith sucked in a deep ragged control of breath. 'No, of course it's not,' she replied, more gently. 'You must never think that. It's because daddy and I are not very happy with each other.'

'But you seemed happy, mummy,' I said doubtfully.

'Yes, well, sometimes things are not what they appear to be. People change. It happens all the time, and where did you get this idea that it's your fault?'

I shrugged, reluctant to admit that I had overheard their conversations.

'Well....?'

'Because you said, you didn't want to come back to Malaya and Aunt Verity thought we should because of me. Now you're angry with daddy, and we have to go back to England again. I'm *always* moving!'

'I know. I know that's how it must seem.' She patted the bed. 'Come here, sweetheart. Come and sit beside me. I shouldn't have shouted at you. I'm just very upset. Our going back to England is not your fault,' she said, putting her arm around my shoulders.

'You see, it isn't only because of problems between daddy and me, there's also trouble with the Chinese people, and the Malayan government has declared, what they call, a state of emergency. Because of this daddy wants us to be safe at home in England.'

'Does that mean there will be fighting here, like in the war?'

'There could be, but this time there will be soldiers to protect the plantation.'

'So daddy will be safe?'

There was the merest hesitation as she replied, 'Yes, of course he will be.'

I sat miserably retreating into my thoughts.

She sought to console me. 'Look, I know how much you'll miss Jean, so I'll tell you what we'll do. Jean is soon to go to boarding school, and when she does she can come and stay with us on her exeats. That way you can still see each other. I shall have to see first if Jean's parents agree with the idea, and if they do, then we'll make arrangements once we are settled at home. O.K?'

I took heart at the chance of seeing Jean on her exeats and smiled my agreement by crossing my fingers in luck at her.

She hugged me. 'You're a good girl. Things will get better, I promise.'

Our meal that evening with Roger was subdued and monosyllabic. There was a change in the way he looked at me, his eyes returning again and again to my face and I felt self-conscious under his scrutiny, 'I'll miss you daddy,' I said, eager to break the troubled atmosphere.

'And I'll miss you too, sweetheart. You'll always be my little princess, no matter what,' he replied, directing a look of recrimination at Faith.

Faith's eyes dropped to her plate with a guilty flush to her face which puzzled me. He attempted to fill the loaded silence that hung in the air.

'I expect mummy has told you Maddy I shan't be able to come home for a while because we have trouble from the Chinese. I have to stay here and look after the estate and the rubber tappers, but I'll write to you, and you must tell me how you're getting on at home and all about your new school. You'll soon make new friends and there will be lots of things to see and do in England that you can't do here.'

'I suppose so,' I replied gloomily.

On finishing our meal of nasi goring Faith said, 'I'd better get on with the rest of the packing as we're off at the crack of dawn tomorrow.'

'Yes, you'll need an early start. I've already arranged for a police escort bearing in mind what's happened to

Arthur Walker on the Elphin Estate.' He waggled his ear to say no more in front of me.

Faith agreed with a worried frown. 'Thank you for that doing that. With this trouble boiling up with the Chinese, the sooner we are out of this country the happier I shall be.'

The following morning the three of us stood in awkward silence watching the driver putting our suitcases into the boot.

Roger turned to us. 'Well I hope you have a good journey down and home Faith. Let me know when you've arrived safe and sound.'

'Yes, of course.' She seemed oddly affected at leaving him.

'Take care of yourself,' she said, giving him a lightly held embrace and kiss. 'Oh and it might be an idea to go back to having Janita to look after you. It will make life easier. Aishah is sweet but not the best of cooks.'

Roger expressed surprise, and I saw a look of understanding pass between them, a coded acceptance of something I had no way of knowing then as Faith moved to make her way to the car.

Roger crouched down and put his arms around me and I cried at leaving him. 'I don't want to go daddy.'

'You will be fine, darling, don't you worry.' He held me close for a long time and then releasing me whispered, 'Look after mummy, for me, won't you, and remember, I love you.'

'I love you too, daddy.'

'Come on, Maddy, it's time to go,' Faith called.

I dragged my feet to the car and clambering onto the back seat, I waved and waved from the window until he was out of sight.

And Faith kept her promise to me that life would get better, I thought, closing my eyes to the sun and remembering the happy childhood days after she met and married Edward, a policeman; a kind and gentle giant of a man who dispensed love and discipline in equal measure to us children, having fulfilled Faith's hankering for a large family by giving her a son and two daughters in rapid succession. Restored to her roots with a busy family life that Faith had missed and craved on the lonely outstation of the plantation, she was content and I'd had the rough and tumble of brothers and sisters, new school friends, and Granny and Granddad who lived a mile or two away. They seemed to have aged in the aftermath of war, but their love for me had not diminished or their funny repartee between each other. How I loved to take a bus over to spend a day with them and find one or other of Faith's brothers and sisters there with the Irish jokes and Jewish humour in full swing. I returned home filled to the brim from the loving family atmosphere and having to bite my lip to stop my reflection grinning back at me on the bus window from the memory of their teasing and wisecracks.

Each month I wrote and received letters from Roger. In simplistic words that made light of the dangers, he would say how difficult it was for him to leave the estate with the unrest amongst the rubber tappers who, being intimidated and threatened by the communist terrorists, were afraid to work on the plantation. He told me I wasn't to worry for now all the locals had been re-housed in new villages in the jungle. They were ringed by barbed wire and had watch towers for protection which stopped the 'bandits' threatening them for food and into joining them. I saw him only twice after leaving Malaya and I was shocked to see he had grown prematurely old, the aftermath from his years of internment and the demands of the emergency. He seemed uneasy with me and it wasn't until just after my fourteenth birthday on a summer's day when staying with Aunt Verity and Maurice in their cottage I discovered the reason why and it shook the foundations of my world.

***

It was a glorious afternoon and we'd decided on a walk to Mousehole. The sea was dancing with stars and the air with the luminescent quality of light so loved by the St. Ives's artists and I felt a rush of happiness to be back in Cornwall again. Verity and I chatted companionably along the sea front, reminiscing on how different it looked during the war with the gun emplacements at the swimming pool, the barbed wire on the beach, and the green turned over for allotments. I laughed with her remembering my impatience to visit the magical island of St. Michael's Mount.

By chance or design our conversation turned to Roger and his family. I'd spent a few days with them before coming on down to Penzance and I mentioned how strange it was that I looked nothing like Roger or his family or indeed, had ever felt I was one of them. It was something that had lain at the back of my mind and crystallized as I grew older. A sixth sense that all was not as it seemed. We were disparate in our physical make-up and temperament. They were dark of hair and eyes and heavy-set whilst I was slim and light boned, my hair strawberry blond, my green eyes flecked with grey, and I had my Jewish nose. I was accustomed to Faith's family's easy going humour, and their hoots of laughter. Roger's parents had a reserve I found difficult to penetrate.

At my saying this, Verity shook her head with a mix of annoyance and exasperation.

'You should not be saying this to me, but to your mother,' she said sharply.

Taken aback at her harsh retort that was uncharacteristic, I stopped and stared at her.

'What do you mean I must talk to mum? I don't understand, Aunt Verity.'

She would not be drawn and said not to press her for it was none of her business and repeated I must discuss it with Faith when I returned home. We walked on in silence and then, as was her quiet way, she took my arm, slipping it through hers saying it was not me she was annoyed at and apologised for snapping at me. I had a sudden hazy memory as a child of her taking me to the fish pond in the Morrab gardens. I remembered I was upset, and then, as now, with an intuitive dart of understanding I realized her anger was not directed at me but at Faith. We smiled at one another, made small talk and I did not broach my suspicions again, determined to enjoy our last few days together.

On the train home, I stared out of the window at the scrubby Cornish hinterland of small fields and burrows with old mine stacks and engine houses rushing by and mulling over Verity's reaction to the question I had asked myself over the years. It clarified into one startling and obvious conclusion. It all fitted, my sense of not belonging, our sudden flight from the rubber plantation; the rhythm of the wheels clickety-clacked the answer, over and over again at me. He's not your father, he's not your father, and was bringing me ever closer to the truth of my birth. I could think of nothing else as I watched the changing countryside, my head filled with a million questions. Who *was* my father? Where did she meet him? Was it someone I knew? How dare she keep it from me. My impatience burned within me on the interminable journey home. At last, after changing trains at Paddington, I finally came into Tottenham Hale station and threw myself off it and walked quickly along the streets to Braemar Road, my temper rising with each step to our front door. I steamed through the house into the kitchen.

'*Why*, didn't you tell me Roger's not my father? He's not is he?!'

In the middle of beating the sugar and eggs for a sponge cake, she blanched at my fierce anger, her eyes wide with shock, her hands arrested in mid-air over the basin. Julian the youngest looked at me with big wondering eyes.

'That's enough, Madeline. You'll upset Julian. We'll talk about this later, when you've calmed down.'

Susan and Becky came running in from the garden, happy to see me home again. I was in no mood for them, and picking up my suitcase, marched out of the kitchen and up stairs to my bedroom.

'What's the matter with Maddy?' I heard Susan say.

'Nothing. She's tired from her journey, that's all,' Faith replied.

I slammed my bedroom door shut and threw myself on the bed and glowered at the picture of Dirk Bogarde looking down at me from the wall opposite. 'And you can stop looking at me, as if I'm a freak, too!' I muttered.

Later, Faith knocked on my door and stood in the doorway. She's as nervous of the truth as I am, I thought, seeing her tense face.

'Can I come in?' she asked.

She perched on the stool by my dressing table.

'What I'm about to say, I should have told you many years ago, as Verity cautioned me to do, and I'm sorry for that. She warned me it would be a shock if you discovered the truth.'

'That's what the row between you was about all those years ago, wasn't it?'

'Yes it was.'

'I knew it was to do with me.'

'You have always been perceptive, even as a small child. Edward says you seem to possess a sixth sense about things. It's true. Roger is not your father. I fell in love with a man called James Treneer. He was a mining engineer who I met at a dinner party. This is no excuse I know, but at the time I was very unhappy because I discovered that Roger had been messing around with other women and in particular with Janita our amah. There was even talk he had a child by her. James was alone because his wife was living at home in England and waiting to join him. Neither one of us set out to be unfaithful but the attraction was instant and we fell deeply in love and you were the result of that love for which I have no regrets. If he had not died in the war, we were going to make a home together.'

'Did his wife know about your affair with him and about me?'

'Not that I'm aware of. He was going to tell her but then the war came.'

'How convenient,' I hit back.

She recoiled. 'Maddy, please—

'I don't want to hear any more of your sordid little affair,' I lashed out. 'I just feel sorry for his poor wife.' I glared at her and rolled away from her pathetic, pleading look.

'Madeline, please try and understand—'

'Oh just leave me alone!' I shouted.

She stood up. 'Dinner will be ready soon,' she said, and quietly shut the door behind her.

So it was true. Roger wasn't my father. I seethed with the knowledge of it. How *could* Faith steal another woman's husband? I would never forgive her. As for

Roger, he was beneath contempt. What love I had for him died, my eyes opened to the hidden sub-text and undercurrent that lay between him and Faith. Roger's actions had set in motion a situation with Faith that escalated into a state of affairs over which he had no control. Between them all they had poisoned my whole existence. I meant nothing. I was nothing. My anger exploded into tears and I lay and cried with the shame of it.

It was if a demon had entered me. I created chaos where calm and harmony had existed, determined to punish Faith, to make her life as dismal as mine. I pushed the boundaries of her patience until it was at breaking point. She tried reason, I was intolerant. She attempted to explain, I became moralistic. There were no shades of grey in this whole sorry mess she'd created. My young bewildered half-brothers and sisters observed I was like a rabid dog, pleading with me to return to the sister who played and read stories to them and was nice! Edward remained solid in support of us both, never wavering, sympathetic to my resentment, sensibly allowing the anger to work itself out of my system. And all the time, deep within me, I hated myself for hating her for loving James, a man I desperately needed to uncover. What did he look like? Was he tall or short? Dark or fair? Did I take after him in looks and temperament? I punished myself. I would not give in and provide her with the satisfaction of my asking.

So much of life had crowded in on me since then. I followed Faith in her love of nursing by training and qualifying as a paediatric nurse and left London and the last flickering embers of a love affair with a man I later discovered was married. How utterly ironic it made my judgement of Faith. I had been well and truly knocked off my moral high horse and from this came compassion and understanding, my teenage rebellion honed and tempered in the fire of experience. Jaded and spent, I was seized with an overpowering hunger for wild seas and the wide open skies of my childhood, and there was a memory that never faded of two little girls standing on a platform.

I pushed myself up out of the deckchair and went to the kitchen to start preparing food for my evening meal. As I sliced and chopped, a picture of Verity and Faith at the table hysterical with laughter over a bottle of port came vividly to mind. I grinned to myself and wondered if Verity remembered that mad and gloriously funny afternoon. Her inebriation was such, I doubted it, but I would still tease her about it when she arrived home next week!

Chapter Seven

I MET HIM in a cabinet-makers workshop in one of the little back streets of Penzance. I had gone there on the recommendation of a friend for I wanted some restoration done to Verity's small table that stood by her chair. He had not seen or heard me entering the work shop, intent as he was on chiselling and shaping a piece of wood. I saw how a wave of thick brown hair fell forward, partly obscuring his face and his impatient flick of it back. He could do with a hair cut I thought flippantly for it grew with the natural curl of the sort that required constant taming, as I knew only too well from Faith's thick corkscrewing hair, and the hours I had spent brushing it.

'H-e-l-l-o,' I sang out. 'Mr. Retallack?'

He sprang back from the work bench, his whole body registering shock and confusion.

'I'm sorry. I didn't mean to startle you.'

'Kitty!' he stammered. 'I thought you were in Malaya.'

'I'm afraid I'm not Kitty.'

Hope that I saw had briefly flared in his face died away as he recovered his composure.

'My name is Madeline Johnson I'd heard you do—

'Did you say *Madeline*?'

'Yes, that's right.'

He stared at me with a look of astonishment.

Puzzled, I became hesitant. 'I have come to the right place, haven't I? You are Mr. Retallack who does furniture repairs?'

'Yes, I am. Forgive me. It's just you took me by surprise. You reminded me of someone I once knew,' he said, looking at me intensely as if absorbing every contour of my face.

'Everyone knows me as Terry, by the way,' he said, wiping his hand down his overall and shaking mine. It was warm and strong, the fingers calloused from physical work and in a curious way, comforting.

'Everyone has a double, or so they say,' I replied lightly, thinking his physical response to my looks had been so immediate that whoever Kitty was must have been pretty special. A coincidence too, that she was in Malaya as I had once been.

'I was wondering if you could repair a small table for me. The pedestal seems to be coming adrift. I'm afraid I don't have any way of bringing it to you.'

'That won't be a problem. I could come and pick it up after work. Where do you live?'

'Not far from here,' I replied. 'Down on the prom actually in one of the cottages there, called 'Seaspray.'

'I know where it is, just along from the swimming pool.'

'Yes that's right.' I felt myself relaxing to his open and friendly manner. 'It's certainly well-named. I remember one night when I was about five or six I was woken up with gale-force winds and waves crashing over the sea wall hurling pebbles against the window panes. The noise was terrifying and in the middle of the storm this man appeared at the foot of my bed with the most wonderful smile that made me feel safe and protected and then he just faded away. For years I wondered if it was a dream.' I stopped, feeling foolish. What on earth had come over me? It was something I had not admitted to anyone. My cheeks reddened at his faintly amused look.

'I'm sorry,' I said, 'I don't normally babble on about storms and ghosts. You must think I'm crazy!'

'Not really,' he replied with an ironic half-smile. 'I seem to have been down this road before.'

'Oh! Have you?' I replied, nonplussed at his remark.

He looked embarrassed. 'Sorry, I spoke without thinking. Ignore it. I'll just get my order book.'

We seemed to be having the most extraordinary effect on one another, I had butterflies in my stomach, and the heat of his touch brushing past me was like an electric shock. His intense blue eyes met mine and my heart leapt to my throat. In them I saw a hunger and empathy too, for he had not shied away from my talk of seeing a ghost. Rather, from his odd remark, I believed he understood. My body zinged with exhilaration, charged and heightened with the sweet scent of wood and camphor, the mix of shavings and glue, oils and polish. This was madness. The signs were painfully familiar and my head cautioned. I had vowed never to be burnt again on love's wheel of emotions after the hurt and loss from my affair with Stuart. Now it seemed of no consequence. I had left his fast moving financial world with a need to reconnect to my dreams and childhood memories of Cornwall. They had drawn me back with gossamer threads, strong as a spider's web. It was here that I belonged.

He arranged to come to the cottage that evening after he'd scratched together a meal, at which he smiled, and said, life was rather ad hoc at the moment living over the work shop, and he was still busy making it habitable since moving to Penzance from Camborne.

He arrived looking with interest around the cottage, remarking on its age and admiring Verity's antique pieces of furniture.

'I'm sorry that was rude of me, but my appreciation of furniture is in the blood!'

I laughed. 'Well actually the furniture is not mine or the cottage. It belongs to my friend Verity. This is her holiday home. She lives most of the year in Malaysia.'

His look of incredulity was such that I could not help but ask, 'Do you know Verity?'

'No. No not at all. I may have heard her name somewhere. It seems vaguely familiar but then everybody talks about everybody in Penzance!'

Despite a hunch he was covering the truth with a joke, our eyes met in laughter and over a cup of coffee we talked with easy intimacy. A current of happiness shot through me when he admitted, with a grin at my probing, he was not romantically involved, and as the early hours of the evening turned into the early hours of the next morning, we both knew we were falling in love. It was as inevitable as the pull of the moon on the tides, and yet, it took us by surprise with its swiftness and intensity. He lit a flame within me that I could no more leave him than leave my own body, and when in my quiet moments I questioned as to whom Kitty might have been and the fact that we were similar in looks, I recklessly cast them aside. Fate or fortune had brought us together and I was like a bird soaring deliriously in the sky, never more alive, never more unaware of how short my flight and the landscape that lay ahead.

Our wedding was intimate, needing only our families and a few close friends at our side. Faith had travelled down from Tottenham with Edward and my brothers and sisters, and Verity who had arrived for the wedding and her summer vacation from Malaysia. She seemed disturbed in Terry's company. 'Don't you like him?' I asked.

'Yes, I do, very much. I'm just tired and jet lagged,' she replied, giving me a hug. 'Oh it's so good to be home again, and you look positively radiant. I've been so looking forward to seeing your wedding dress. It sounded simply beautiful from your description on your letters. So come on then! Where are you hiding it?'

I realised Verity had neatly side-stepped and distracted me from any further questioning when later on I came across them speaking low and tensely in the garden. On my appearance they stopped and pretended all was well between them and suggested a walk along the prom. Something did not sit right with them both and although I tried prising it out of Terry, he was like a clam and there was nothing I could do about it for I loved them both and did not wish for any ill feeling to mar our wedding day. At the altar, Terry turned to greet me with such a depth of love in his smile it radiated every pore of my being and I was borne away on a cloud of happiness. We were one and nothing and no-one could separate us.

We were busy decorating the living room when I found myself asking the question.

'Why don't your parents like me, Terry?'

'Don't be silly, darling, of course, they like you. Why shouldn't they?'

'I wonder that myself. I haven't got two heads! All I know is when I'm around looks pass between them as if they know something I don't. Who was Kitty?' I asked, the question coming from some deep intuition within me. 'You said I reminded you of her when we first met.'

He avoided my eye, busying himself with opening and stirring a new tin of paint. 'She's someone I knew when we were children. We grew up next door to each other. There is a resemblance to you which mum and dad will have noticed, but I don't see why that should affect their relationship with you in any way. If it bothers you that much, I'll speak to them about it when I next see them.'

'No, don't do that, Terry. It would seem like a criticism and I have no wish to cause bad feeling between us. After all, we did take them by surprise getting married so quickly. Given time, when they've come to know me better, I'm sure all will be well, especially when our baby arrives.'

Terry's face lit up at the thought of his unborn child. 'I have to confess darling, I'm hoping it's a boy. I've always wanted a son to show him how to make things, as dad did for me. We used to disappear together down to the shed at the bottom of the garden. We'd be gone for hours until hunger drove us back to the kitchen where Mum was usually baking. Her pasties were the best in the west. Still are!' he laughed.

'Verity and mum used to make them when we lived here in Penzance during the war, but they were never up to the mark of your mother's. Then again, it was war time, fat for pastry making was scarce and the amount of meat hardly worth taking home.'

I stood back to consider the colour of the first coat of paint on the living room wall of our terraced house in a quiet backwater near the Morrab gardens. Yes, it was just right. Like the softest blush of a Cornish sunset.

Chapter Eight

I SAT AT the kitchen table gazing absent-mindedly out of the window overlooking the courtyard and small back garden and ruminating on the recent discovery that our home had a resident ghost. I would hear her laughter, her light footsteps running up the passage way from the kitchen. Sometimes when reading or listening to the radio, we saw the door handle turning into our living room and felt the temperature drop, no matter how high the fire roared in the grate. The ghost child was mischievous. Things would mysteriously move which brought accusations to each other of not putting things back in their place.

'Have you seen my fountain pen, Maddy?'

'The last time I saw it, it was on your desk,' I replied.

'Well, it's not there now!'

I found my gold locket given to me by Terry on our wedding day glinting on the settee.

'It must have slipped off when you were wearing it,' Terry said when I scooped it up with a cry of relief that I'd not lost it.

'No, I definitely put it into my jewellery box days ago and haven't worn it since because Robert has been making a grab for it when I'm holding him.'

Keys which we dropped into the wooden bowl on the hallway table would mysteriously disappear only to turn up on the kitchen table top, or on the sideboard, creating a doubt in our minds that we must have set them down there without thinking. And then the penny dropped. It had to be the little ghost child playing tricks on us. Often I fancied I could see her out of the corner of my eye, like a sunbeam of light. At first we laughed at her pranks, but after frantically searching for the door keys one morning to go out, only for them to reappear back in the bowl, I began to lose patience and to be disturbed by her presence.

'We have to do something about it Terry,' I said to him that evening. 'I think perhaps we should have a word with the Minister on Sunday. He might be able to suggest the best way to deal with it by cleansing the house with holy water and prayers, or whatever it is they do in these circumstances.'

'That sounds a bit drastic. She's not malicious, just rather mischievous. She doesn't bother me at all. Ghosts seem to follow me around,' he quipped with a grin.

My jaw dropped. I had not expected this.

'You look surprised,' he said.

'Well I am. I thought you'd be in agreement with my suggestion. And what do you mean, ghosts follow you around?'

'Oh nothing really, just a silly remark. I've never seen one but they do occasionally seem to become part of my life, that's all. Actually,' he said, rapidly changing the subject, 'as I've caught up on the orders for my furniture, I'd like to take a day or two finding out the history of the house and the people who lived here. After all, we've always assumed our ghost is a little girl. For all we know it may well be a boy.'

If I hadn't known him better, I thought, his usually open and honest face was, in point of fact, looking a little shifty, and, I realized, when he left the room mumbling that he must chop up some firewood, he *still* had not answered my question.

With his mind made up, Terry cut himself some sandwiches and took himself off the next day to the

Morrab Library. Converted from a Victorian mansion it was a private library with a wealth of Penzance's history and its district in thousands of books. Terry often visited it for it had the comfortable air of a gentleman's club with large rooms, leather chairs for quiet reading and desks at which he studied the old designs of chairs and tables to adapt with fresh and innovative blueprints for new furniture. It stood in the grounds of the Morrab gardens, a semi-tropical park that was popular with sheltered seats in leafy recesses for lunchtime breaks, a feast for the eyes of colourful flower beds and a bandstand for Sunday's entertainment. It was a fair assumption Terry reasoned to Madeline that their house being built in the eighteen hundreds would be recorded there, and if it proved necessary, he could chase up more about the family by seeing the Parish and Census records. Two days of patient research and he had found out all he needed to know and more from a very helpful assistant librarian who impishly revealed, along with facts and figures, the local gossip of the once wealthy families of their area.

Terry dropped his notes on our old pockmarked wooden kitchen table, pulled a chair back that screeched in protest on the slate floor and sat down. He loosened his tie and watched as I put the potatoes on to boil, and began to slice a Cornish hogs pudding to fry with an egg for dinner.

'Well, I found her. And it didn't take as long as I thought it might. You were right darling. Our playful little spirit is a girl. Lucy Trevanion born in 1896, died in 1903 at the age of seven from scarlet fever, poor little soul. Children stood little chance of recovery in those days. The librarian told me there's always been talk of our house being haunted which inevitably made it difficult to sell. Those in the know steered clear of buying it and it stood empty for quite a while, until we came along! That could explain the very reasonable price we paid for it,' Terry said with a wry look. 'Anyway, Lucy was the only child of a seaman, one Captain John Trevanion. It was rumoured he did a very profitable trade in smuggling that enabled him to build the grand three storey house we now live in. He got a bit above himself with the gentry though who mocked him for thinking himself bigger than bully beef! Unfortunately, he got his comeuppance for his nefarious ways, as Miss Peters quaintly put it, in a very sad way. He lost both his wife and his daughter. It was said he was never the same man after that. He sold up and moved to Mousehole where he lived a simple life in one of the cottages behind the harbour front, earning his living with a small fishing boat and a line for mackerel fishing for the tourists and hotels.' Terry laughed. 'I daresay a lot of what she told me was fancy. You know how we Cornish love to embroider things, but it made for an interesting morning!'

So now I knew the ghost child's name. Lucy. I could sense her when she was around and it seemed so did our baby son Robert, who at six months sitting up in his high chair, often stared fixed and wide-eyed at something in the kitchen. I wondered if he was seeing the little girl and had the urge to discuss it with someone other than Terry and could think of no-one better than Verity who was coming that morning to take Robert out in his pram. She was home for the summer months and took to popping up from her sea front cottage to our sunny facing terraced house. There was a knock on the door. She was here. I tucked in his coverlet and opened the door.

'Right, he's all set to go!'

Her smile was one of pure delight. Verity, utterly smitten with Robert from the day she set eyes on him, cooed and clucked as I handed him over to her for his daily constitutional down to the sea front and back up to the Morrab gardens where she liked to sit in a sheltered nook and enjoy the flower beds and sub-tropical plants which were out in a riot of colour.

Robert slid his hand to the side of the pram and dropped his rattle onto the hall floor. A game he loved to play. Verity picked it up laughing and shaking it at him. 'You are a little rascal,' and handing it to him he promptly threw it out again and chuckled at her.

I gratefully took the breather from the baby routine and decided to clean the third story of our home, and empty out boxes of Terry's work papers stored in the room and sort them away into the filing cabinet there. With its turret window letting in a flood of light, Terry thought it perfect to use as a studio for his drawings and furniture designs. His business was growing rapidly in the post-war years when people were looking for something new and innovative. Word had spread of his flair for putting a contemporary stamp on traditional furniture as well as his restoration of antique tables and chairs and it became necessary for him to take on Colin, a young and eager-to-learn apprentice for his bespoke creations. I hummed a popular tune to myself as I ran up the stairs.

On entering the room I stopped dead for the rocking chair, left behind by the previous owners, was in motion, rocking gently to and fro. Lucy was up to her tricks again.

'I know you're there Lucy,' I said, looking at the empty chair. 'Are you surprised we found out your name?' and feeling self-conscious at talking into thin air I walked to the window and stared out across the gardens to the sea beyond. A thought parked at the back of my mind a long time ago was nagging away, and it had been triggered by Terry's remark about ghosts. My thoughts ran on to our first meeting in Terry's workshop and my garbled tale to him of seeing the ghost of James at my bedside. How crazy it must have sounded. And what did he mean by his reply? "Not really. I seem to have been down this road before," And now this last off-the-cuff comment that "ghosts seemed to follow him around, although having never seen one himself." It was a strange thing to say. I couldn't shake the feeling of a sixth sense of warning I was missing a clue. With my mind mulling it over, I began to empty out the boxes of pattern books and blue prints, drawings and sketches, and after filing them away, I brushed up the floor and dusted ready for Terry's work easel and desk. I checked my watch. There was no more time to dwell on the mystery of ghosts for Verity would soon be back with Robert.

'Even Robert seems to be aware of someone else in the room,' I said, spoon feeding him in his high chair his pudding of mashed-up bananas and custard. 'Do you think he can see Lucy or is his stare just what babies do?' I asked with a nervous laugh, apprehensive as to how Verity would receive my tale of ghostly happenings in our house.

Her reply took me totally by surprise. Of all the people I knew, I would not have taken Verity for a believer in the supernatural, and it was the reason I'd confided in her for a more rational explanation.

'Have you ever read that lovely poem by Wordsworth *Intimations of Immortality* where one of the lines says, *heaven lies about us in our infancy?* Verity asked with a loving look at Robert. 'I think Wordsworth must have had the same conviction as me that young children are close to the spirit world. How often have you heard of parents saying their children have an imaginary friend? Mostly they ignore it thinking it's a phase the child is going through, or they are told not to say such things, or even they are lying. This is hurtful to the child and a pity because as the physical world manifests itself more and more into their consciousness, so the door closes on spiritual mysteries. That's my belief, anyway. I've come to accept such happenings as ghosts, premonitions, psychic phenomena, call it what you will, because of the experiences of a friend of mine and Maurice's encounters with the paranormal. Maurice was very down to earth, but his experiences in the war changed his way of thinking and he came to accept the inexplicable.'

'Who was the friend? Someone I know?'

Verity looked caught off guard and gesticulated dismissively. 'No. Just someone I met whilst in Malaya after you'd left,' she said casually. She turned and clucked at Robert, 'Who is Aunt Verity's beautiful boy then?' and handed him his rattle. He bestowed upon her a beaming smile, and I was left with the niggling impression she was hiding something from me.

I lifted him from his high chair and sat him on her lap, where she could not resist kissing the soft hollow at the nape of his neck, breathing in the baby scent of him mingling with Johnson's soap and powder. 'He's so gorgeous Madeline,' she said, 'I could eat him up! He's going to capture all the girls' hearts one day.'

Watching her, I grinned and said, 'He already has. Yours and mine! I find him an endless source of joy and wonder. He's such a happy baby. He smiles on the world and his infectious gleeful chuckle never fails to set Terry and me laughing. We've nick-named him 'smiler.'

'You know, sometimes when I'm holding him he looks at me very intently with those blue eyes of his father and I wonder what thoughts lie behind them. He probably thinks he's been landed with a mad woman for a mother with my talk of ghosts!'

'Not only you!' smiled Verity. 'I'd make a bet he thinks we're both mad as March hares! And just look at those eyes and that smile of his….

'reeling us in, hook, line and sinker!' I said with a grin.

Chapter Nine

Malaya 1968

KITTY LOOKED FOR Lawrence in the melee of women in a room set aside in the bride's family home for the start of the Muslim wedding ceremony. She saw him with his camera focused on Ming who sat wearing a full length cheongsam of white silk brocade with decorative fastenings of gold braid frogs. Her long black hair swept up and away from her petite features was held with a seed pearl and silk flowered headdress. Kitty thought she looked as small and exquisite as a Chinese doll.

The sound of the Kompang drums heralded the arrival of Ahmad beneath a yellow umbrella and escorted by men bearing gifts on copper trays decorated in tiered arrangements of orchid flowers. He came into the room and Ming shyly accepted his offer to her of a token sum of money, the *mas kahwin*, that sealed the contract of marriage between them.

She and Lawrence had met Ahmad when their infant daughter Amy had fallen ill with a fever. As the company doctor, he had arrived at speed to attend to her where they lived on the mining camp of Tronoh Mines in Malaya. The rapport between them had been instant, and a close friendship was quickly struck up with him and his fiancé Ming and the invitation to their wedding was an honour rarely given.

Kitty watched the ceremony performed by the Kadhi, the religious official of the Syariat Court with a mixture of happiness for her Chinese friend and a deep sense of despair that threatened to overwhelm her.

Her thoughts returned to her own marriage day four years ago. She was as happy then as her friend was now, deliriously so. Why had it gone so disastrously wrong? Did Lawrence feel so unsure of her love that it had driven him to drink? He was certainly jealous of any conversation with their male friends. That had been made abundantly clear at the club's Christmas party last year. It had been the most humiliating day of her life. Fuelled with drink, he practically marched her out of the club room. Once in the car, she was stunned at Lawrence's preposterous accusation of her flirting and dancing closely with Graham, the amiable manager of a nearby rubber plantation. Graham's amusing anecdote had died on his lips at the sight of Lawrence's face when he returned with the drinks, and he sprang from his chair beside her like a startled doe. And yet, when Verity had come to stay with them Lawrence had proudly boasted that Kitty was like a mother hen with the bachelors, inviting them around for a meal as they needed the civilizing company of women to prevent them going bush! Or was he still running scared of her gift of second sight, despite confirmation from Verity, time-slips could and did happen?

His ridicule was nothing new. She had experienced it with her school friends when first she spoke of seeing ghosts. At first curious, they eyed her like a strange specimen, nervously asking her questions and giggling uneasily at her replies. They called her the 'ghost girl' behind her back, all except Terry who lived next door, and whose memory she immediately pushed away. She quickly learnt not to speak of the people she saw but when Lawrence questioned the number of times he found her staring fixedly into space, and suggested that she might be suffering from Petit Mal, she could no longer be evasive. Kitty confessed to him that all her life she'd experienced seeing things from the past. He had reacted as she had feared with disbelief and insisted on her seeing a doctor. When his examination proved fruitless, as Kitty had warned Lawrence it would, he became petulant and took to taking frequent drinks from their new cocktail cabinet. She had been delighted when he had purchased it for her one Christmas with its custom made matching occasional tables of honey coloured teak with delicately carved banding of flowers. Now she wished she had never seen it for he repeatedly returned to the cabinet to replenish his glass from a variety of liqueurs and bottles of whisky and brandy. It was the poisonous mix of beer and whisky she feared the most. Evenings became a trial of nerves with the atmosphere turning toxic as the drink took effect. Reeling around her chair and waving his arms in a parody of a ghost, he looked down at her in distain as if she were a mad dog. Kitty shrank from his ridicule and was terrified his drink-fuelled anger would overspill into violence against her. So far only inanimate objects had felt the weight of his rage but the fear it would escalate stalked her day and night. The closeness they once shared in the tropical nights was gone. Where they had played a game of cards or chess, quietly read, or listened to music before going to bed to make love, now became a battleground and the joy she felt from the mystical union of oneness in their love making died within her leaving Kitty desolate.

Bewildered at the sudden change in Lawrence, in desperation she confided in her friend Maggie for she had no way of judging the effects of alcohol. Her only experience of drink was at Christmas or special occasions at home with her family when they might become a little merry but she had never seen anyone descend into such anger.

'I've noticed he does drink rather a lot, Kitty,' Maggie admitted. 'It needs to be nipped in the bud before it gets completely out of hand. Some men do become belligerent and violent with drink. Don't let that happen to you. Others, like my husband are filled with bonhomie and gradually slide into sleep snoring like a foghorn!'

She was jolted out of her thoughts by the crowd moving apart for Ming and Ahmad to process to the sitting-in-state ceremony where their elders came to bestow upon them gifts of money, the blessings of long life and happiness with the sprinkling of petals and scented water, and eggs that symbolized a fertile union. The children in their colourful clothes waited patiently for their turn, offering little pouches of sweets.

The strict segregation of the sexes at the beginning of the ceremony was now relaxed for the wedding meal. Kitty sat with Lawrence upon large carpets and Indian rugs covering the floor of the living room which had been opened up with the folding back of dividing doors. Long runners of white tablecloths were laid down on the carpets in preparation for the food, which now began to arrive, a feast of colours, textures and aromas in bowls and plates piled high: delicious beef randang, nasi lemak chicken with yellow coconut rice, prawns in a rich sambal sauce, and ikan masam manis, a fish with a sweet and sour sauce. There were dishes of mixed vegetables tossed in vinegar, and puddings of pineapple in a thick sweet kerisik sauce, slices of fruit and Kitty's favourite, gula malacca, a mould of sago with a jug of sweet toffee tasting syrup and cool coconut milk. Kitty saw Lawrence's grimace when a glass of soft drink was placed before him and felt only relief. He would have to wait a few more hours before the evening reception when the rules of drink were relaxed.

Sitting on the other side of her, Ming's brother-in-law, Dominic, an Australian, turned to introduce himself, asking where they came from and their connection with Ming and Ahmad. Kitty's replies were hesitant, guarded, looking to include Lawrence, and Dominic caught an unmistakable signal from him, a flash of grey cold-eyed warning from the man beside her. He had experienced it before, men with beautiful women whose fear of losing them became a need to control. Her green eyes mesmerizing in their clarity, looked away from Dominic with a smile, but behind them, he detected a meloncholy something deep and unspoken. On turning back to Lawrence, who draped a possessive arm around her shoulders, Kitty's long golden-red hair was caught in a shaft of sunlight, setting it into a halo of fire and Dominic thought she was the most unsettling woman he had ever encountered. Her eyes seemed to see into his very soul.

With the family wedding ceremony over in the bride's house, Lawrence and Kitty took their leave and drove home to change for the formal reception in the groom's residence, an evening dance of celebration when foreign associates and friends of both families came together.

Lawrence slipped the car into gear and moved swiftly from the driveway onto the road.

'Who was that man sitting beside you?' he asked with a sour expression she had come to know well from his drinking. 'He certainly took your obvious attributes in.'

Kitty's spirits sank. She had hoped her brief words with Dominic would have passed without comment, and had done her utmost to include Lawrence, would have introduced him, had he but given her the chance. She ignored his cutting remark, deliberately keeping her voice light and conversational.

'He is Ming's brother-in-law, Dominic who's Australian. Isn't it amazing how every one of Ming's brothers and sisters have married out of their race? It's so unusual, especially for a Chinese to marry a Malay. It was like a gathering of the United Nations! The only other Chinese we know who has done that is Maggie's husband Cheng Moi. Did you know that he met Maggie in Ireland where he went to finish his education?'

'No, I didn't actually.'

'Maggie said his mother, the matriarch of the family, was a right dragon when she arrived in Malaya, and a dead ringer for the lion in the Chinese New Years lion dance!' Kitty chuckled. 'Maggie does have a way with words.'

Lawrence could not help a reluctant grin. 'Well contrary to popular belief that the Chinese women are subservient, it is, more often than not, the wives who rule the roost and hold the purse strings.'

'Really!? Well, it must have been even more of a shock then when Cheng Moi turned up, not only with his qualifications in engineering, but with an Irish wife in tow. He knew his mother would never have approved of him marrying outside of his race, so he married her in Ireland. Fate accompli. Apparently, she treated Maggie like an unpaid servant until the children started to come along and they were given a house of their own on the mining camp. All the resentment died down, and like all Chinese grandparents, they dote on them. There's nothing like a baby for healing divisions.'

'Is that a dig at me, Kitty?'

Kitty did not rise to the bait. 'You know it's not.' She laid her arm across his shoulders with a soothing tease of his hair at the nape of his neck. 'I thought the Muslim wedding was so colourful and exotic, didn't you? I feel very privileged to have witnessed it. Ming looked beautiful. I hope the photographs you took turn out OK. There was quite a crush around her.'

Lawrence mentally shook himself. He had to stop this gut-wrenching irrational jealousy. Why had he become like this? Kitty had done nothing to deserve his suspicious mind. He caught her hand, kissing it, and held it lightly in his lap.

'Yes, Ming did look lovely, but for me, on our wedding day, you were simply stunning. I couldn't take my eyes off you.'

He saw Kitty's smile in response did not reach her eyes.

His stomach lurched in alarm. 'We are happy aren't we, Kitty? You know I would never do anything to hurt you.'

'I know, Lawrence,' she replied softly, gazing out of the car window thinking but that's what you're doing, and the tragedy of it is, you're not even aware of what's happening between us because of your need for drink. In the silence that followed, Lawrence reflected on their rows about his drinking. They were beginning to get him down. What was so heinous with having a drink or two after a day on the dusty open-cast mine? A thirst quenching Tiger beer cooled him down and relaxed him. With a drink in his hand, life felt good and when out with friends he'd feel foolish not accepting the offer of a beer or a glass of wine with a chaser or two of brandy or whisky. Drinking was simply a way of life out here. It hardly merited Kitty's accusation he was turning into an alcoholic.

On the night before leaving Malaya to return home for her confinement, Kitty had warned him she had no intention of bringing their child up in the venomous atmosphere created with drink inside him. His behaviour terrified her and she feared his violence. It was a shocking admission and one he found hard to believe, for he had no recollection of his snarling anger the following day. The break from each other would do them good, she said; give him time to take stock, decide which was more important, drink or his wife and their soon to be born infant.

The ultimatum had brought him up sharply. He loved Kitty deeply. How could she even think he would physically harm her, he asked? Again and again, he pleaded how sorry he was, swearing he would never touch another drop. He took her into his arms, murmuring how much he loved her, so much so, he had given her the child she craved, although she knew he had never felt, as other men did, that burning desire to have children. Kitty was unmoved. A strong maternal instinct with a need to protect her unborn baby had created a core of steel within her, leaving him with an icy pit of fear. He was trapped between the love for his wife and the need for the demon drink. An apt description if ever there was one, he thought.

On driving home after seeing Kitty off at Kuala Lumpur airport he had resolved to cut back on his drinking. He must not, could not, lose Kitty. She was his life. God knows in the interim period after she had flown from KL, and before he had arrived in Cornwall for his three months leave, he had done his utmost to lay off the bottle, but the world was full of temptations; company cocktail parties, going home parties, kind invitations from friends to dinner whilst he was on his own, and once home, every pub in Cornwall beckoned him.

***

98

With Kitty's time entirely taken up with the day and night routine of their newly born infant, there were times he was at a loose end, and he took the opportunity to steal away for a quick pint at Tyacks, the local watering hole for old and new mining students from the Camborne School of Mines. Kitty looked up at him from nursing Amy. He saw the unspoken plea in her eyes.

'I promise I will only have a pint of bitter, or better still, a shandy. If I was seen sporting a glass of orange juice by old students, they'd think the tropics had softened my brain, which it probably has,' he grinned. 'Sorry, not a joking matter, I know, darling. See you later.'

He had been careful, knocking back a few quick pints of beer and steering clear of whisky, a mix that he knew pushed him over the edge. He kept himself on a tight rein at home, was attentive to Kitty and the baby, a model of a husband and proud father to her family who were around every day to dote on their first grandchild. Gradually Kitty's wariness disappeared. She dared to trust him again, was the Kitty he remembered, teasing him with her laughing eyes, full of joy and love for their daughter, Amy, who, judging by all appearances was going to be as lovely as her mother. It gave him a wave of satisfaction. She drank her milk, slept, was passed from arm to arm without a murmur, and contrary to previous experience of friends' infants whose looks held no attraction other than to the gushing parents, Amy's features were fine with skin the blush of a peach. He had succeeded in keeping the drinking under control. Life was back on an even keel. Kitty had been making a mountain out of a molehill.

Tronoh Mines came into view, and they swept through the gate opened by the Sikh jaga to their house on stilts. The gardens of the houses on either side of them were open with green lawns and the bright splashes of the red and yellow of canna flowers and hibiscus. On their veranda, pink and purple bougainvillea spilled over the pots where rattan chairs and small glass topped occasional tables stood. Ah How, their amah, came to the door with Amy.

'Everything OK Ah How?'

'Yes, mem. Amy had her afternoon nap and has been pushing around her baby walker. Would you like me to prepare her tea?'

'No, I'll do that today. You go and have your meal. I'm afraid we're later back than we anticipated and we shall be going out again this evening.'

Amy, who was just eighteen months tottered towards them, her golden curls catching the sun. Kitty lifted her daughter to swing her around, laughing and kissing the silky softness of her face. Lawrence walked swiftly to the kitchen for a cold beer and Kitty's laughter died away.

She followed him and watched him snap off the bottle lid and sitting in his chair he quickly poured and downed the beer.

'I needed that,' he said. 'It's been a long afternoon sitting on carpets in a very dry desert. I'm going to get another. Did you want a drink?'

With her stomach churning with tension and in an effort to keep her voice mild she asked him for some freshly squeezed orange juice from the fridge and could not stop herself from saying,

'Don't have too many beers darling, the evening is going to be a long one and knowing how generous Ahmad and Ming are, the drinks will be flowing.'

'For God's sake, Kitty! It's hard luck if a man can't have a drink or two without being held to ransom,' he snapped.

'But it's never just a drink or two, is it, Lawrence?' Kitty replied, with despair and resignation in her voice. 'Do you think I don't know of your little tricks. Orange juice in your glass to hide the smell of spirits, your sneaking out for surreptitious night caps when you think I'm asleep. Are you really so blind to your drinking that you think I can't smell it on your breath?'

Lawrence stared at her. It was clear that over the weeks Kitty had not been deceived with his subterfuge, had probably guessed he kept a store of bottles locked in his office cabinet.

His resentment at the knowledge she had not been fooled, erupted. 'You're making me sound like a criminal. If I fancy a drink, I shall have it. I don't have to ask your bloody permission!' He jumped up angrily from his chair and made for the kitchen.

'I can't take much more of this Lawrence,' she cried after him. 'You need help!'

Lawrence slammed the fridge door shut. 'What's that supposed to mean?' he retorted, refilling his glass.

'Exactly what I said. You need help. I've kept hoping you'd come to your senses, but it's never going to happen is it? Please talk to Ahmad, Lawrence. They may have such things as AA meetings here like they do at home.'

Lawrence glared at her. 'You're unbelievable. I don't need the dammed AA. Just because I like to have a drink, it doesn't make me an alcoholic any more than you consider yourself mad when you have these 'so called' visions of the past? If anyone needs help around here, it's *you*. It certainly isn't me!'

Amy's bottom lips trembled at their raised voices. Her blue eyes swam with tears.

'Stop shouting Lawrence, you're frightening her.'

'I didn't start this. You did. All I wish for is peace in my own home. And I get precious little of that these days.'

Kitty's patience snapped. 'If that's the way you feel, Lawrence, well I know what to do.' She lifted Amy from her chair. 'Come on sweet pea. Mummy will give you a bath. You can play with your new duck.' She turned on her way to the door. 'Whether you like it or not, this is going to be sorted, one way or another.'

'Fine!' he called at her retreating back and opened the cocktail cabinet. 'Do what the hell you like!'

With a deep sense of foreboding Kitty swung her legs into the car. She had begged Lawrence to let them use the Company's driver for the evening but Lawrence, bitter with her awareness as to the extent of his drinking and her veiled threat of leaving him, was in no mood to listen. He was perfectly capable of driving his own damn car and would be drinking whatever was on offer at the wedding and if she didn't like it, she could stay at home. He would offer her apologies to the bridal couple and Ahmad's parents, saying she had suddenly become unwell and was unable to attend the reception.

Why oh why hadn't she done just that? she thought, sitting back in her seat and shutting her eyes.

The evening turned into a tight-rope of emotions and fraught with anxiety as Lawrence accepted a steady flow of drinks from the waiters mingling amongst the guests. She was fearful he would descend into another bout of angry exchange with her, or worse still, with a guest. She made an effort to calm herself with the thought that to date, he had always been careful not to lose control in public. That would come later, for her, when they were alone. She watched Lawrence working the room of the cosmopolitan mix of Ahmad's parents' business associates, friends and family and was struck

102

anew by the aesthetic beauty of him. His height gave him a striking presence with his sand-coloured hair, his clean-cut features and deep set grey eyes. It had not been hard to fall in love with him. She remembered the dances in the village hall, the young girls bowled over by his easy charm, his flattering attention emboldened some to become flirtatious, and the more timid to be tongue-tied at the force of his personality. She had been neither, but had challenged him with a fire and strength he had been unable to resist. Sadness overwhelmed her again. How could he allow his desire for drink to destroy their happiness?

The strain of the evening was telling on her and she was developing a splitting headache. She was anxious to leave, seeing the tell-tale signs of the change in him before he became the worse for drink. She pleaded her headache to Lawrence, praying he would not argue to remain and was grateful when Ahmad caught her eye and come swiftly to them and she explained her need to leave early. She saw Ahmad's flicker of irritation with Lawrence and his softening look of sympathy for her and it struck her like a hammer blow. He *knew*. But his natural courtesy and reticence to a friend and foreigner in his country forbade any sign that he was aware of the problem, and she felt sick and humiliated that he had seen through Lawrence and his drink-ridden destructive self-deception.

On pulling away from the house, the wedding lights strewn along the driveway lit up the gold of Kitty's long brocade dress and her pear-drop diamond earrings glinted and flickered against her neck. Lawrence glanced at her sitting silently beside him, beautiful and glacial as ice. Before all this censorious nonsense of his drinking she would have shared the memories of the evening, her eyes sparkling with happiness and laughter, but now she was as cold as the diamonds at her neck. He was being treated like a pariah. A sudden tide of fury sent an adrenaline rush of blood through him. Well, if this is the way things were to be, so be it. He pushed his foot hard down on the accelerator. They were now out and away from the town and on the long winding road to their mining camp. The dense blackness of the tropical night enveloped them and the headlights of the car picked out the trees at the roadside like looming spectres. Kitty could see the speedometer swinging to ninety miles an hour and her heart was pounding with fear.

'Please Lawrence, slow down! You're frightening me.'

Lawrence's laugh was crazed with drink. 'I thought you liked speed, Kitty.'

'Yes, but not like this. This is madness. You know how dangerous this road is at night. Lawrence for God's sake slow down!' she screamed, as a sharp bend came to greet them.

With a screeching of tyres the car careered off the road and glancing off a tree reared up, tumbling over and over with the banging and buckling of tortured metal. The sounds of the crash carried to the tappers houses before being swallowed up by the thick canopy of rubber trees. They came running to find Lawrence dead in the mangled car and Kitty lying unconscious amongst the trees.

She was floating like a cloud through pure white light with golden rays enveloping her in the warmth of a summer's day, and from dancing silver orbs the most beautiful music flowed through her like a soft breeze. Ethereal beings shone around her like pulsating beams of light, and she could see the earth glowing with a vibrancy of trees and flowers rich in colour and clarity. She was soaring in a world of wonder, suffused with indescribable joy and a feeling of such peace and love she never wanted to leave and cried out when it vanished, leaving her desolate and shaking with fear and pain at the top of a dark tunnel.

'No! No! I don't want to go down there,' she screamed, sliding into its blackness.

There was the touch of hands, the same gentle hands that lifted her from the depths of the sea. Her silvery voice was whispering in her ear. *'I am here. I am always with you.'*

Chapter Ten

'IS THAT MRS. Pengelly?'

'Yes. It is.'

'My name is Martin Cooke from Personnel of Associated Mines in London. I'm afraid I've got some rather bad news about your daughter Elizabeth and her husband Lawrence Scott-Thomas.'

Octavia felt her bones turn to water at the sympathetic voice at the end of the line. This couldn't be happening to her, not again. She felt faint and disbelieving. Her Kitty in a coma? Confusion and fear swirled within her. 'When did this accident happen?'

'Yesterday evening. We have just been informed of it.'

'And Amy. What about Amy, my granddaughter? Was she in the car too?' Octavia's voice rose with fear.

'No, and she's fine Mrs. Pengelly. She's with Mrs. Scott-Thomas's neighbours, a Robert and Wendy Parker?'

'Oh yes, I recognize the names. Kitty - we call my daughter Kitty - spoke of them.' Octavia struggled to think coherently. She felt sick to the pit of her stomach. 'And Lawrence's parents? Do they know?' she asked, as the enormity of the news of his death began to sink in. 'I must ring them.'

'Look, Mrs. Pengelly, this must be a tremendous shock for you. Is there someone who could be with you now? Is your husband at home?'

'No, I'm afraid he died three years ago.'

'Oh, I'm so sorry to hear that. Someone else perhaps, a friend or neighbour?'

There was only one person Octavia knew that she wanted at her side. 'My sister May,' she replied.

'That's good. We can talk about this further, tomorrow, when we have more information. We have informed Mr. Scott-Thomas's parents about his death. I know it's hard but please, try not to worry. What you must keep in mind is that your daughter is alive, and although very ill at the moment, she is not alone. She has a friend who says she will be with her every day. A Mrs Verity Nicholls and of course, staff from our office in KL will be keeping in close contact with the hospital.'

'Thank you, that's very comforting to know. Kitty has mentioned Mrs. Nicholls. She's a friend who has stayed with her on the mine.'

'Now, Mrs. Pengelly,' Martin Cook continued kindly. 'May I suggest you put the kettle on, make yourself a strong cup of tea and see if your sister May can be with you for support. Rest assured, we are doing all we can from this end and will keep you informed of Kitty's medical condition and the eventual arrangements for her flight home. We will ring again tomorrow, and will also be sending to you details passed to us from the hospital as soon as we receive them.'

Octavia, moving like an automaton, did as she was bid, filling the kettle and spooning tea, how many she knew not, into the pot, and with her legs giving way, sat down heavily in the old wooden arm chair by the kitchen range. How strange. She had done exactly the same thing the day that Kitty was born. It was rather battered now. The chair had seen her through so many desolate days with its soft cushioned back and seat that gathered her into its comfort. Then it had been the District Nurse bustling around to make her a cup of tea before preparations for the birth of Kitty. She remembered how the thought of tea churned her stomach. Like her stomach was turning to bile now.

'Oh Kitty,' she moaned quietly, 'I can't lose you too.' She was shivering and cold as ice. She pulled the heavy embroidered shawl from the back of the chair, a gift from her eldest sister Alice in Greece, and wrapped it around her shoulders.

She sat and waited for strength to return to her body and her thoughts went back to the bitterly cold winter when Kitty was born when the snow was so deep that nothing moved and the lifeblood of the land was silenced, taking with it Kitty's twin sister and leaving Kitty fighting to live at just three and half pounds. She did not stir nor cry nor give any sign of sentience until the trees came into leaf and the sun was sending shafts of smoky gold through the lime green leaves onto the carpets of bluebells in the woods, and hastening the country lanes to burgeon into life. Only then at six months was Kitty ready to greet the world, to become a child who sensed and saw things that others could not, and who was to Octavia an eternal mystery with her talk of angels and ghosts and her uncanny instinct for sensing people's troubles.

How can I take care of you as I did when you were a baby? You're as far away from me as your father James was in the war and who died before ever seeing you. Her breath caught in a shuddering sigh. So many deaths she had faced and now, Lawrence. The grief, she knew, would consume his parents. He was their only child, their raison d'etre. Her heart went out to them.

How did the accident happen? It was difficult to keep her thoughts from running wild imagining Kitty lying broken and half-dead amongst the trees; Lawrence lifeless in his car.

Hysteria bubbled away inside her. She must not give way to it, but stay calm. Kitty was alive. She must keep telling herself that. They would be doing all they could for her out there and Amy was safe and sound. She had that to be thankful for. The kettle whistled. Octavia rose, poured the boiling water into the pot and covering it with the tea cosy, left it to brew and with a feeling of unreality walked from the kitchen to the telephone in the hall and rang her sister May.

May, the youngest of William Tremayne's four daughters was making saffron buns and absent-mindedly singing under her breath when the memory of Kitty popped into her mind. She smiled remembering the little girl dancing and jigging around her kitchen to the jingle '*If I knew you were coming I'dave baked a cake*' that May always sang to her when Kitty landed on her doorstep. Of all the times for the phone to ring it would be when I'm up to my armpits in saffron dough, she thought. She hastily rubbed together her floury hands and walking to the hallway humming her signature tune for Kitty, she picked up the phone with sticky fingers.

'Hello May....' Octavia broke down.

'Octavia, is that you?'

'Yes. Oh May, something terrible has happened.'

Octavia's voice sounded faint and strained, quite unlike her decisive self.

'What do you mean, something's happened?'

'It's Kitty.......'

Thoroughly alarmed, May cried out. 'I was just thinking about her. Is she alright?'

'No, she isn't.' Octavia's fear and panic was palpable down the phone. 'She's been in a car accident. She's in a coma and Lawrence is dead,' she ended abruptly.

'Oh my God. When did this happen?'

'Yesterday evening, I think. I dunno. I can't remember.'

'And what about Amy. Is she hurt?'

'No, thank God. She was at home with the amah.'

'Look. I'm on my way. Don't do anything until I get there,' although quite what she thought Octavia was going to do, she could not imagine. May hurriedly rinsed her hands, covered the dough and putting it on the shelf over the warmth of the range to rise, she threw on her coat and half running, half walking along the road from the outskirts of Camborne town, she silently pleaded. Please Lord, not this. You cannot take Kitty too. It would be a loss too far for Octavia to endure; so many deaths. Was it to never end? Fear lent her wings. She flew up the steep hill and along the terrace to Octavia's house and fell breathless through the back door.

In spite of her state of shock, Octavia could not but help a weak smile. It was a replay of the war years when Kitty was born; May at nineteen rushing in through the back door from her shift at making aircraft parts in the engineering firm of Holmans, and without stopping to hang up her coat, hurrying up the passage to check on Kitty lying in her cradle by the fire kept burning night and day. Kitty had always been close to May, almost like another daughter to her. On the odd occasion when a dart of resentment needled her, Octavia at once felt ashamed. How could May be other than close to Kitty. She had been with her since the day of her birth, shared with Octavia her grief over the loss of Kitty's twin sister, and on that unforgettable day at Gwithian beach, had saved Kitty's life. But for May, she would have drowned.

May poured a cup of tea, and pulled a face. It was practically black. 'I know you like tea strong as bark, Octavia, but this is ridiculous!' she exclaimed, pouring it away down the sink.

'The man from Personnel told me to make a strong cup of tea, so I did,' Octavia retaliated. 'Does it really matter?'

'OK, OK, keep your hair on!' May made a fresh pot and pouring herself another cup sat herself at the kitchen table. 'Now what exactly did they say about Kitty?'

'Nothing more than I told you on the phone. All I know is she's very ill and in a coma. I feel so useless. She's half way across the world from us, all on her own. I should be with her.' She swallowed the threatening tears. She would not give way. She must stay strong and in control.

'The Company did say that her friend Verity Nicholls was at her bedside which is good to know. They also said they would be making arrangements to fly her home. But when will that be? I know nothing about comas. She could be weeks, months, depending on her injuries.'

May gazed reflectively down at her tea and shook her head in disbelief. 'I just can't believe this is happening. Lawrence   speak ill of the dead, but I was never that fond of him. Thought a little too much of himself for my liking and I've always suspected he had a weakness for drink.' She shot a guilty look at Octavia at her tactlessness. 'I'm sorry I shouldn't have said all that. '

For a moment, Octavia lost her despairing air and looked sharply at May. 'What are you saying May? That Lawrence was an alcoholic?'

'No, of course not.'

'Then what made you say it?' Octavia persisted.

May felt pinned like a butterfly and shifted uncomfortably on the chair. Why could Octavia never let things rest?

'Well….?'

'It was just little things I noticed when they were home with the baby. How anxious Kitty became when he went out for a drink with friends at Tyacks, and when we wet the baby's head at the christening, she touched his arm, as if to say, enough.'

'I see.'

'Look, I feel terrible. I don't know what made me say those things, and I'm probably way off beam. Forget it. I'm not thinking straight with this awful news about Kitty. I wish we knew more about her condition.'

'They said they will be ringing me tomorrow with the hospital report.' Octavia's thoughts raced with dread. 'What if she doesn't come out of it, May. What if she dies? I can't go through that agony again. I just can't,' she cried out.

May moved swiftly from her chair, and crouching down took her hand and looked gravely into Octavia's frightened blue eyes.

'Kitty is not going to die Octavia. She's going to be alright. Gosh, your hands are cold. It's the shock.' She began to rub them between hers. 'You mustn't even think that. Kitty is young and strong and has been a survivor from the day she was born. Remember how minute she was, she was smaller than her teddy. She looked like a skinned rabbit!'

Octavia nodded with a faint smile at the memory. 'Yes, she did, didn't she? I used to call her that. My little skinned rabbit.'

'I must admit I had my doubts she would pull through those first few months,' said May, 'but she did and has survived more hair-brained scrapes than any child I know, and that includes my Helen. Do you remember that day at Gwithian? She had been under the water for so long, I thought we'd lost her, and then, up she popped from the depths of the sea right beside me. It's something I shall never forget Octavia, never. She said her guardian angel saved her, and I for one, believe her and come to that, so did Jack. I know you've always thought it silliness but Kitty has a strong belief in the power of the spirit, and this will pull her through, you mark my words.'

Octavia stared blankly at the top of May's head, as May stirred life into her cold hands.

'You've always had such pretty hair May. You ought to show it off more. Try a different style.' She went silent watching May kneading her hands. 'Why does this keep happening to us, May?' she asked abruptly.

May shook her head wordlessly, realizing Octavia was thinking of another car accident, one that had killed their mother. When barely in their teens, she had saved their lives by pushing them away from herself and from an out-of-control car careering down the hill backwards on the main street of the near-by town of Redruth. The horror of it still lay unspoken, heavy and pregnant between them. May wished that Octavia could let go of all that emotion and fear that was so obviously boiling away inside her with the devastating news of Kitty, but tears were a side to Octavia she had not seen since their mother died. She buried grief deep these days after James's death in the war, and the loss of Kitty's twin sister at birth and dear Jack three years ago. If there were any tears left, May was not privy to them.

The tragedies had fused the sisters like nothing else could into a closeness not displayed in their childhood. May's sunny and easy-going nature contrasted sharply with Octavia, who practical and down-to-earth, ruled her household with a will empowered by the calm submission of Jack. If only Jack were alive to give his strength and support to Octavia, thought May, who had always loved him for his special kindness to her after their mother died, when for a while she lost the power of speech and her mind. The unexpected death of Jack had knocked the family sideways. He had been a part of their lives ever since he had started working as a clerk under their father William, Registrar of the School of Mines until he had died, when, as a natural progression, Jack had stepped into his shoes. May had often suspected Jack's love for Octavia for his eyes never left her from his desk in the corner when she and her sisters went in and out of the School's office, and his face betrayed his depth of feelings on seeing the flash of her diamond ring on her engagement to James.

It was at a war-time Christmas gathering arranged by Octavia and May in their home a year after James had died that Jack seized the day and asked her out to a Bob Hope picture in the local cinema. To his surprise, she accepted. Octavia found his fierce intellectual mind coupled with a keen sense of humour an irresistible combination and his gentle attentive courtship bore fruit for in the autumn of 1944 when Kitty was three years old, they were married and the following year Kitty was presented with her sister Grace, to be followed within two years by her brother Thomas.

Octavia took heart from May's words, looking at her plump and sweet faced sister fondly over her freshly made cup of tea and remembering her whirlwind courtship to Ted, a clerk in the bank of their hometown of Camborne. Young and wildly in love they had impetuously set a wedding date before his call-up to the war in North Africa. Impulsive and scatterbrained she may be, she thought, but when it came to the crunch, May was there for her, could be relied on. They had lived together and weathered the deprivations of war and watched over Kitty growing from an infant, scarcely alive, into a happy, active three year old who ran around between them like a fair haired little doll, until she had married Jack, and on Ted's demob, May left to settle with him like peas in a pod in a terraced house near the engineering works of Holmans. I keep my own counsel, thinking its strength, but was it really, thought Octavia? She knew people respected her, listened to her sound advice and judgment, but it was May, the open book with a lightness of spirit they loved.

'Let's move upstairs and sit in the bay window of your bedroom like we've always done over the years Octavia, in good times and bad. The sunshine and view over the fields to the sea will help to calm us down, make us feel a little better.'

May, dropped her cup and saucer on the small low table in the window and sat opposite Octavia. Below them the town of Camborne lay hidden by the trees of the manor house of Nancarrow: a bustling thriving town resulting from the tin and copper mines of Cornwall down through the centuries. Octavia thought of Kitty's letters home saying she missed the strong sense of Cornish community with its social activities and festivities connected with their church and the engineering works of Holman Brothers, whose foundry hummed with the noise of a workforce of thousands; men in machine shops making precision tools, boilers, pumping engines and all manner of subsidiary equipment for mines around the world. Women worked above them in a room of clattering typewriters and in the director's offices, were the ancillary clerical staff. Each year Holmans and Camborne town celebrated together with bunting and music, contests and dances, and with exotic entertainment of Cossacks and circuses from around the world. Octavia could only hope and pray those memories deep in the recesses of Kitty's mind would pull her back from the coma.

'Heavens! I've just thought. Who's looking after Amy?' asked May.

'The amah who Kitty said she would trust with her life, and Kitty's neighbours Wendy Parker and her husband. I forget his name. They have two little boys. They arrived a few months ago and Kitty was delighted for now she had company during the day whilst Lawrence was out on the mine.

'That's a relief. Still, poor little soul, she must be wondering where her mummy and daddy are'.

'Yes, and it grieves me not to be there with her. The man from Associated Mines said that Kitty's friend Verity Nicholls would be visiting every day and the staff from the office in KL would also be keeping in close contact with the hospital. I was so relieved to hear that. I would go quite mad if I thought there was no-one with her at all. Kitty does have other friends she has written about on her letters. There's a Maggie who lives on a neighbouring tin mine, and a married Malay doctor and his wife Ming.'

'Yes, Kitty has mentioned them to me, as well.'

'The only problem is,' Octavia went on, 'they all live in the Ipoh area so I would imagine it won't be easy for them to visit Kitty, if at all, with her being transferred to a hospital in KL.

'Have you rung Thomas and Grace yet?' asked May.

'No, I didn't want them thinking they should come home to be with me. There's nothing anyone can do for now. I shall wait until I have more details tomorrow.'

'And we shall have to break the news to Alice and Phoebe,' said May. 'It's times like this I wish the family lived closer, what with Alice in Greece and Phoebe the Lord knows where....'

'Yes, it's a pity we're so scattered, but in any case, all they or we can do is hope and pray.'

Chapter Eleven

VERITY WAS SITTING in the suite of her hotel room enjoying her morning coffee with the New Straits times when the words leaped off the page.

"On the evening of the 20th May, Mr & Mrs Lawrence Scott-Thomas of Tronoh Mines were involved in a car accident on their way home from a friend's wedding. Mr Scott-Thomas was tragically killed outright and his wife is now in a coma at the Assunta Hospital. Their baby daughter who was at home with their amah at the time is temporarily in the care of their neighbours, Mr and Mrs Parker of Tronoh Mines."

Horrified, her hand flew to her mouth. 'Oh dear God,' she whispered. Lawrence. Dead? And Kitty, so beautiful and spirited, now barely alive it seemed. She could scarcely take it in. She moved swiftly to the phone. She must ring the hospital.

She had first met Lawrence and Kitty in the hotel where she had taken up residence. On her way up to her room after an afternoon's bridge party, Verity happened to glance into the faded grandeur of the dining room. It was empty, as it frequently was these days, apart from a young couple now sitting in the corner by the dais that once bounced to the energetic music of orchestras and jazz bands. Verity remembered when the room buzzed with life, the dance floor crowded with men and women from the civil service enjoying Saturday night's entertainment, the planters and miners from out-station propping up the bar and ranged around smoky tables

117

littered with drinks clinking with ice. She took a step back down the stairs and looked again. The young woman's figure was familiar and there was no mistaking her strawberry blond hair. Good heavens! It was Madeline! Without thinking she propelled herself quickly across the room and lightly tapped her on the shoulder.

'Madeline, my dear. What are you doing back in KL?' she asked.

Kitty turned around in surprise and Verity equally astonished, stepped back. Verity could hardly believe the resemblance to Madeline. It was uncanny.

'I'm so sorry,' she flustered. 'I'm afraid I've mistaken you for someone else.' How could she have been so foolish, she chided herself? She knew full well Madeline was busy working as a nurse in Penzance, and on her return there asked Verity if she could rent her cottage until such time as she found a place of her own. Verity assured her nothing would give her greater pleasure. It had been and was her home for as long as she needed it.

Lawrence and Kitty exchanged pleasantries and when Verity commented she rarely saw Europeans in the restaurant these days as they had migrated to the newly built and luxurious Merlin Hotel for meals and world wide entertainment, Lawrence, recently graduated as a mining engineer, had invited her to join them for dinner. She discovered they were not long married and had just arrived from England and were in transit to travel up north to the Tronoh Mines near Ipoh. The liking between them was mutual and over the meal Verity related to them her life in KL before and during the insurgence and the difference in the religions and cultures of the diverse races. She explained she had recently lost her husband Maurice and having made a home in Malaya for more years than she had lived in

118

England, and with no living relatives there, had settled on the idea of taking rooms in the hotel to continue to enjoy the company of her wide circle of friends. In the English summer months when Malaysia was at its hottest, she returned to her holiday cottage in Penzance, an arrangement she said that gave her the best of both worlds. Lawrence and Kitty exclaimed at the coincidence of them also living in Cornwall and despite their brief acquaintance, Kitty with her strong intuition that their meeting was no coincidence, had kept in touch with phone calls and in the following year invited her to stay with them on the mining camp in Tronoh. It was an unforgettable visit where family secrets were revealed from a photograph of Kitty's and she had learnt of Kitty's physic abilities to see into the past. She also sensed all was not well between Kitty and Lawrence and saw his predilection for drink. It did not bode well and now this....

On first seeing Kitty in the hospital, Verity was horrified. She was unrecognizable and Verity was thankful that Octavia was not there to see her. She would be distraught at the swelling to her face and head, her eyes purple and puffed from the bruising, her leg in plaster and traction, the saline drip and intravenous tubes coming out of her body. She felt tears spring to her eyes. Her first letter to Octavia was not going to be an easy one. It was a miracle she was alive.

Martin Cook of Personnel, sympathetic to Octavia's distress and desire to be with Kitty proved to be efficient and good as his word. He set up a liaison between Verity and Octavia, explaining to her it would put Kitty's mother's mind at rest to know from a friend of her daughter that she was having the best possible care. Wheels were set in motion for the surgeon to give the details to Verity of the gravity of Kitty's injuries.

She had sustained a fractured leg and arm, two of her ribs were broken but had not punctured her lungs, and a ruptured spleen had required immediate surgery. Her injuries were life threatening and the trauma to her head was causing them significant concern. On asking him when she was likely to come out of the coma and would there be lasting damage, was told it was a case of wait and see. She was young. The body has strong recuperative powers. It was this hope that Verity clung onto and would write to Octavia.

Kitty stirred and moaned.

Nurse Chin assigned to Kitty with a sweet and gentle way that belied a maturity and knowledge beyond her years took a hypodermic needle from a tray.

'Mrs Scott-Thomas I'm going to give you something to take the pain away.' Nurse Chin administered the injection and reassured Verity it would work quickly to calm Kitty down.

'Her nick-name is Kitty,' said Verity. 'I was wondering, do you think it would assist in Kitty's recovery if all the medical staff called her by her nick-name?'

Nurse Chin considered Verity with understanding eyes. 'You are a good friend to Kitty, Mrs Nicholls. Yes, I think it's an excellent idea and I will let everyone know. We believe anything that might bring a patient back from a coma is always worth trying.'

Sweet release. She was whirling back into brightness and was filled with happiness to see Terry coming towards her. He took her hand and led her away from the dark tunnel of the coal shaft of Nancarrow Manor where they had broken in, and up the steps from the cellar. They went out and along a flagstone passage past a vast kitchen, cool meat and dairy rooms, and through a baize door into a large marbled-floor entrance hall where a grand staircase curved away to the rooms above. They drifted in an out of rooms, high and spacious with ornate fireplaces and luxurious furnishings and where eyes from oil portraits of men and women frowned down upon their intrusion. A ladies escritoire in the window caught Kitty's eye but just as she reached it, in an instant it was gone and she was standing in a library with a full length Gothic window giving out onto an Italian garden with a fountain. It was a gentleman's room smelling strongly of pipe smoke, an intimate room with books ranging from floor to ceiling with a leather arm chair in which to read by the window. The sun outside created rays of coloured light to fall from the heraldic glass onto a magnificent mahogany pedestal desk with a tooled green leather top where a family photo stood. The lady wore a long dress and picture hat and standing each side of her were two boys in quaint old fashioned clothing and a girl in a dress of ribbons and flounces. With an intake of breath she recognized them. They were the ghost children she had seen in the garden when she had hidden behind a rhododendron bush and watched them clambering into a boat in the Victorian boathouse.

'Look Terry, these are the children I was telling you about. You see! I wasn't making them up.' She wheeled from the desk to find Terry had gone.

'Terry! Where are you?' she cried out in panic. 'Don't leave me here on my own.' She spun from room to room frantically calling his name. Where was he? She *had* to find him for there was something she desperately wanted him to know. Had she left it too late to tell him she loved him still?

It was mystifying how light she was, light as thistledown, and quick as a thought, she was in the nursery with Terry sitting astride a rocking horse. On the children's table was the musical box, so familiar to her that she ran to it instinctively. She cranked the handle to listen to the tinkling harp-like notes of *Silver Threads Amongst the Gold* and then the music changed to the sound of thumps and the terrified cries of children. She turned ice-cold and was fighting to breathe in a nightmare of a spinning black void and crying, crying for Terry.

Verity who was reading at Kitty's bedside, shot out of her chair at Kitty's sudden thrashing around, her breathing a strangulated gurgle, and with fear snapping at her heels ran to find Nurse Chin, and barely knocking or waiting at the Sister's office door rushed in to find her and an intern in consultation on a patient.

'I'm sorry to interrupt' Verity cried in panic, 'but please come quickly Nurse Chin. Kitty seems to be choking.'

Nurse Chin and the intern moved with such speed, brushing Verity aside in their running to Kitty's room that she was momentarily left standing, before adrenaline rushed through her veins and she ran after them where she found the doctor removing her tracheal airways tube and administering a sedative injection. Kitty became very still.

'She's not dying is she?' Verity whispered in dread at her death-like stillness.

Nurse Chin was reassuring. 'No, Mrs. Nicholls, on the contrary, she is now breathing for herself, it is a good sign.'

Verity's legs went weak with relief and she sat down abruptly.

'I will get one of the auxiliary nurses to bring you a cup of tea,' Nurse Chin said with a concerned look at Verity's pale face.

'That's very kind of you. Thank you. It was just the fright of seeing Kitty like that.'

'Of course. It was very understandable,' Nurse Chin replied with a sympathetic smile. 'Now that Kitty is in a semi-conscious state, you will find she will switch between restlessness and passivity. It's quite common with a head injury. Sometimes patients become aggressive through confusion, other times they wake up briefly, often talking incoherently and fall asleep again, so don't be alarmed it's all quite normal.'

Verity did as the nurses suggested, talking to Kitty despite her deep sleep, for they believed patients could hear, and anything to help the cognitive awareness and understanding of things going on around her was good. By keeping in close contact with Kitty's neighbours, the Parkers, she was able to tell Kitty the little things that Amy was doing, trusting that somehow it would stir a memory of her daughter. She told her amusing stories of friends at afternoon bridge or mahjong, and recounted her stay with Kitty on the mine.

Kitty had been in the coma for a week and in despair at the lack of any indication of improvement, the doctor explained that patients could take weeks, even months to regain consciousness and sometimes, regretfully, they never did. With Kitty he felt the signs were hopeful as the swelling to her brain was diminishing. The thought of Kitty so engaged with life, so overjoyed with her baby daughter, and who might not ever regain that awareness, filled Verity with such sadness she renewed her determination to do all in her power to bring her back into the world that Kitty loved.

She leant over her sleeping form and kissed her softly and holding Kitty's hand tightly as if to instil her own animating force into her.

'Do you hear me Kitty? You are going to come out of this. I will take you and Amy home to Cornwall to be with your family. You *will* get better.'

It was a decision so right and quickly made, it surprised even herself. It gave her a purpose after the ease, and, if she were honest, the meaningless filling in of days since the loss of Maurice that still caught her heart in grief in unexpected moments. She would leave Malaysia for good and live in her cottage in Penzance in the rugged beauty of Cornwall, and within easy distance of Madeline and Kitty who she looked upon as the nearest to daughters she would ever have; two people she had come to know and love in the most extraordinary of ways.

Kitty struggled to look through the slits of her eyes. She blinked at the brightness of the room; saw pale blue curtains floating down the windows. Someone was lightly holding her hand.

'Terry?' she whispered.

Verity could feel alarm flexing through Kitty's fingers.

'Kitty, it's me, Verity. Don't be afraid.'

Verity? Who was she? 'Where am I?'

'You're in hospital, Kitty. You've been in a car accident.'

A blurred face appeared over her with the sing-song intonation of the Chinese.

'Hello, Kitty. So you've decided to return to us.'

Kitty was out of the coma and Verity's heart sang with it. Kitty had said a name. Terry! The boy she knew as a child. It was the first sign of awareness, and the doctors cautiously agreed, it was a start. She wondered as she entered the imposing entrance of glass windows soaring between two square blocked pillars and walked along the gleaming corridors of the Assunta Hospital known for its excellence in nursing care, what the odds were of her meeting both Madeline and Kitty at such disparate stages in their lives. She remembered Kitty with her mystical ways once saying, "There's no such thing as coincidence. Everything in our lives happens for a reason in its own allotted time and space." Be that as it may, she was privy to family secrets that should not be hers to keep and the fact did not sit easily on her conscience. Acting as loco parentis to Kitty and keeping Octavia apprised of Kitty's progress by phone and letter, she was glad to do, for heaven alone knew the worry and anguish the poor woman must be going through, but the thought of meeting her with the knowledge that Octavia had no idea of James's affair or of his daughter Madeline and Verity's close bond to her, filled her with apprehension.

"*Oh what tangled webs we weave,*" thought Verity on entering the coolness of the air conditioned private room where Kitty lay. Kitty smiled at Verity, a face she did not remember but which became familiar from her daily visits. Verity longed for some sign of her recognition of Amy whose photograph the Parkers had sent down, and which she left propped up to face her on her bedside cabinet. It seemed Kitty had forgotten everything of life in Malaysia, for when awake, she did not ask for Lawrence or Amy but spoke haltingly of Terry, her siblings Thomas and Grace and her mother, and when remembering her step-father Jack, a tear would trickle down her cheek.

At eight weeks with her bones beginning to knit, the decision was reached that it was in Kitty's best interests to now fly her home for assessment in a London hospital before returning to Cornwall. Verity made her regular call to Octavia, saying that Kitty was slowly improving, and she would be greatly pleased if Octavia and the Company permitted it, to chaperon Kitty and little Amy home. She gently warned her that Kitty's prognosis was uncertain for on emerging from the coma, Kitty had difficulty in co-ordination, her attention span was short, and she was slow in thinking and speaking.

What Verity did not express to Octavia was how the essence of life had been sucked out of Kitty. Her eyes that once shone with the brightness of a jewel were lifeless leaving Kitty with a melancholic air. It was evident too she had regressed into childhood. She had hoped against all the odds Kitty would improve, but the outcome from the accident was becoming clear. Things were never going to be the same again. The old Kitty had gone.

***

The Associated Mines team with whom Verity came into contact from time to time in hospital understood the circumstances to which Verity now found herself, and, grateful that she would be accompanying Amy home, had pulled out all the stops. Flights were booked for herself, Amy and Kitty and a nurse to attend to her medical needs, and who on arrival would safeguard her to the Royal London Hospital.

The Parkers brought Amy down to KL to stay with Verity in her hotel rooms for the final few days before leaving Malaysia. They said Amy had been asking for her mother and father and young as she was, they thought it best to be honest, explaining to her that mummy was in hospital and that daddy had gone to heaven. At this, Amy had become unnaturally quiet, and sat most days, playing and baby-talking to her doll and clinging to the one constant left in her life, the amah. She looked up at Verity with round blue eyes and was so like Kitty, it made her heart weep. On the Parkers leaving, tears began to well, turning into a noisy wailing cry of abandonment. Verity swept her up in her arms, kissing the top of her golden hair and rocking her.

'You're missing your mummy, and feeling very frightened Amy, I know, I know, but you're safe with me,' she crooned until Amy's sobs became little gasping inhalations of breath.

'My name is Verity and I'm going to look after you. Tomorrow I'm taking you to see your mummy who's poorly in hospital. You'll like that won't you?'

Amy gazed back at her with a tear streaked face. 'Mummy,' was all she said.

On settling her down for the night, a small figure lost in the vastness of a double bed with her solemn face looking up at her, Verity slipped off her dress and slid in beside her. She had never been more conscious as she was then of the vulnerability and fragility of life. She wrapped her arms around the child entrusted to her until she fell asleep clutching her bed-time teddy.

It was with trepidation that Verity took Amy into the hospital. On seeing Kitty, she slipped Verity's hand, running to the chair where Kitty sat and struggled to climb up onto her lap and into her mother's arms.

Kitty stared down at her in bafflement, then across to Verity. 'Whooo isss sheee?' she slurred.

Amy, bewildered at the lack of response, for Kitty made no move to hold her, looked up at her mother with wide uncertain eyes.

'Mummy doesn't understand who you are Amy,' she said, taking her gently from Kitty, and sitting her down on her lap Verity felt a great weight of sadness. She rocked her to and fro, murmuring, 'You see, poor mummy had a bang on her head, and it's not better yet.'

Yes, challenging days and months lay ahead, she thought. Her heart went out to Kitty's family. Far-reaching adjustments would have to be made for Kitty was returning home with the mind of a child.

Chapter Twelve

OCTAVIA'S SISTER PHOEBE watched the two women meeting for the first time in a bond of friendship formed from their shared worry and love for Kitty. Verity held Octavia who finally gave way to the luxury of tears. Over the weeks Octavia had spoken of her fears to Verity as she dared not do to May and the family. She could not allow a chink in her armour or to crumple under the strain, it would only have added to their anxiety. With barely time to say hello to her granddaughter she was hurried away into the ambulance with Kitty and they were taken to the Royal London Hospital.

Phoebe took Octavia by surprise by taking leave of absence and organizing through the Foreign Office a flat for them to stay in until Kitty had been assessed and insisted she would be driving them home. Octavia was touched that Phoebe had taken such trouble for unlike their eldest sister Alice who wrote copious letters of family life in Greece, she and May heard little from her. With the Cold War dangerously bubbling on, they believed her to be still working for intelligence as she had during the war, a fact she never confirmed or denied. As May waspishly observed, the powers that be couldn't have picked a more ideal candidate for covert work for even as a child one never knew what went on behind her cat-like eyes and any secrets would be sealed tight as a gin! Nevertheless, Octavia was grateful for Phoebe's efficient organization for she was shocked to the core at seeing her daughter in such a pitiable state and found London disorientating after the unhurried way of life in Cornwall.

Phoebe was a tower of strength, taking them to and fro to the hospital, cooking them meals with a relaxing glass of wine after the stress of hospital visits. The neurologist after numerous tests came to his conclusions and assessment of Kitty. He was sympathetic and honest, and made it very clear to Octavia the long term implications of a head trauma. Kitty was severely handicapped by specific problems in speech, thinking, behaviour and in social skills. She must be prepared for the idea that Kitty might survive for years totally dependent on those around her. He would be transferring her to the Royal Cornwall Infirmary in Truro for intense physiotherapy and from there it would be advisable for Kitty to be admitted into a nursing home for convalescence and rehabilitation. It was a sobering conclusion.

***

Verity sat at the dining table in Octavia's sitting room and set her mind to put misgivings to one side and concentrate on the pleasure of eating one of Octavia's pasties. Octavia who noticed how tired she looked on her return from Malaysia and thoughtfully allowed her time to recover from her flight and the weeks at Kitty's bedside before inviting her up for a pasty lunch and to chat over Kitty's progress at Truro Infirmary.

It was plain how much Kitty's sad state weighed on her mind. She also found Kitty's observation of Octavia was right. She was not one to easily reveal her feelings although it was evident how grateful she was to Verity for her steadfast care and for bringing her home.

'I simply can't thank you enough for all you've done for me and the family, Verity. The worry at times was overwhelming and your phone calls and letters were a lifeline. Without them I think I would have gone insane. You could not have done me a greater kindness.'

Verity batted the air. Please, don't even think about it. I was only too glad to be there for Kitty. I'm very fond of her.'

'And on her letters to me, she was of you. I was just wondering if you would like to visit Kitty on a regular basis once she's transferred to Nancarrow? You'd be welcome to a pasty, after which we could walk down the hill together to see Kitty in the afternoon. I thought it might help Kitty to regain some memory of her time in Malaysia when she knew you there. At the moment, all she remembers is her childhood.'

'I'd be delighted to Octavia. I agree with you the more Kitty sees of people she knows, the better her chance of recovery.'

On Verity's enquiry as to where Amy was, Octavia's eyes brightened and her bearing lifted with the thought of her granddaughter. She became animated. 'Oh, Amy's living with my sister May.'

Verity registered surprise.

'It was May's idea. After seeing how ill Kitty was, she quickly realised my looking after her and a toddler would not be easy for me. May felt it would be a more settled life for Amy, particularly at the moment with me visiting Kitty on a daily basis, if she was with her and Ted initially until Kitty is home and sufficiently well enough to look after herself. Not only that, there's Helen, their daughter. Although she's working, she lives at home and is on hand to help with Amy. Of course it would be different if Grace and Thomas were still living here, but Grace is married and living in

Falmouth, and Thomas is a teacher and lives in Bristol. Anyway, we decided on Amy coming to me for a couple of nights a week so that she can visit Kitty, and become happy and familiar with both our homes.'

Verity nodded. 'That makes a great deal of sense.'

Octavia's face shadowed with sadness. 'How quickly the years go by. Before you know where you are, they have all flown the nest and then, without warning, one broken bird returns home. Of course, we hope and pray her recovery will not take too long and then Amy will live here with me and Kitty, but I think I fear it's going to be a long haul.

What she could never admit to Verity, and was now deeply ashamed of, was the breach that had taken place over May's idea for Amy to live with her and Ted, and her insistence that Kitty should go into Nancarrow. For a while it split their close alliance with May arguing that Nancarrow was right on their doorstep and held memories for Kitty that might trigger her mind back into the present. Octavia was totally opposed to it, feeling that despite the changes to Nancarrow, and her own antipathy towards it, it would not be the best place for Kitty either who had a fear of the house as a child. For certain, it did not have a happy history. May had surprisingly dug her heels in and stubbornly refused to be swayed by Octavia.

'You have to stop this paranoia about Nancarrow, Octavia. Yes, I know it does have a bad reputation for accidents to the Killigrew family and James's sister died there of course, but the past is the past and the most important thing is Kitty's welfare. Never mind your fears. It's a convalescent home now and a good one. And as the doctor said, it might well be conducive to restoring her memory. It won't be for ever. In time, she will return home to you. But for the moment,' May pleaded, 'you must let her have the specialist care that Nancarrow can give with its extra help of occupational therapy and physio and speech therapists coming in from the hospital. These places are few and far between. It's the best option. Well, the only option, really.'

'So you keep telling me.'

'The other thing is,' May continued, unstoppable in her eagerness to impress upon Octavia the rightness of her reasons, 'Kitty will need to see you, every day if necessary. Her childhood is all she remembers. By the sound of it, it's going to take a long time for Kitty to recover her physical abilities as well as mental and I will do all I can to help and support you. In fact, if you wish,' May said, impulsively, 'Amy could come and live with me and Ted. It would—'

May's words froze at Octavia's angry stare. She had listened to May's verbal battering against her own preferred wishes for Kitty for long enough, and her proposal for Amy to live with her was the final straw.

'Oh I *see*. Is it not enough for you that I've lost our mother, James, Jack and the twin? And with Kitty's husband gone, who you admitted you never liked or trusted, you now want to take their daughter, my grandchild away from me!'

May was stunned. 'I can't believe you just said that,' but Octavia hadn't finished.

'And what about Ted? Has he any idea of this? Or have you been planning it with him behind my back?'

At this, May exploded. 'Oh. For heaven's sake Octavia. It was a sudden thought and if you had let me finish, I was going to say it would be difficult initially for you to look after a toddler as well as Kitty but now I know what you really think and feel about me, forget it. Do whatever you want to. You always have. I'm going home!'

May sprang from her chair and picking up her coat and hat from the hallstand, threw them on, and banged the back door hard behind her. Octavia felt the vibration from the sitting room and Amy who had been quietly sitting on the carpet playing with her toys jumped and began to cry.

The ensuing silence had gone on for days until Octavia could bear it no longer. She must resolve the situation and arrange to meet the hospital doctors in Truro and speak with them again about the idea of Nancarrow as a nursing home.

In meeting with them they spoke with confidence and assurance. Nancarrow house would not upset Kitty for it had been substantially altered, and, surprisingly, said going back to a place of trauma could often work to the doctors and patients benefit. Not only that but the gardens and woods held happy memories for her. All of which might induce a positive response. With such overwhelming confirmation from all quarters in favour of Nancarrow, Octavia felt she had little choice but to agree to Kitty convalescing there. With the decision made, she delayed no longer. In all their years together such an upset had never happened before and she could not deny it. It was her fault. She had to heal this awful estrangement from May.

Octavia put Amy into her pushchair and leaving the house took herself down the hill and out along the road past Holman's Engineering Works. It brought back memories of a young May at nineteen working in the factory on aeroplane parts for the war effort, and reinforced her guilt and shame at her behaviour as she remembered May's thoughts were always for Kitty when she returned home exhausted from her shift. At the end of the Holman's building, she crossed over the main road into the quiet street of houses where May lived.

May opened the door and looked at her warily.

'May, can I come in?'

May stepped back and Octavia walked past her with Amy into the sitting room with her heart thumping, and stood in trepidation of her reception.

The atmosphere was wintry and there was an awkward pause.

'Are you going to sit down, or what?' May asked and waited. She was glad Octavia had come and broken the silence between them, but for once she did not intend to make it easy for her. Not this time. The hurt was too deep.

Octavia's features worked with tension. 'May I'm so sorry for what I said,' she burst out, her voice brittle with emotion.

'It was unforgiveable. I don't know what came over me. I truly didn't mean it.' Her legs suddenly felt disengaged from her body and she sat down with a thump into the arm chair.

At her chalk white face, May felt a reluctant measure of sympathy. 'You've been under a lot of strain, Octavia, and you were overwrought.'

'Yes, I know, but that's no excuse. Can you forgive me?' She pleaded, searching May's face. 'I hate to be like this with you.'

'It hasn't been a picnic for me, either. I've had better moments,' May replied, 'but we've gone through too much together to end up like this.'

Octavia sensed with relief a yielding in May. 'And you were right. The doctors also think Nancarrow will be the best place for Kitty.'

'Well, that's good to hear,' she replied, thinking how hard it would be for Octavia to admit to that.

'And I've come to realise your idea for Amy to stay with you is also a good one. It makes a lot of sense. You forget how busy toddlers keep you,' she admitted with a small confessional laugh. 'That is of course, if you'll still have her, and Ted agrees.'

'Well, he will take a bit of persuading after your performance,' she said.

Octavia winced at the sting.

May had learnt to handle Octavia's temperament from childhood, her need to be in control, although she also knew that beneath her unsentimental exterior she would crave forgiveness. She did not reach out to give her a forgiving hug for that was not Octavia's way but offered an olive branch.

'Look, let's try and forget about the upset. I'll talk to Ted and see if he'll agree to us taking Amy and if he does, another idea might be for Amy to stop over with you for a couple of nights every week. That way you can take Amy to visit Kitty and she becomes familiar with the routine and is happy with both of us.'

Octavia's mercurial sea blue eyes beneath her short jet black hair held May's warm hazel ones with a mixture of remorse and relief.

'That sounds ideal May.'

'Well now that's settled, would you like a cup of tea?'

'I could certainly drink a cup. My mouth is dry as a bone and I'll take Amy out of her pushchair and sort out a drink for her.'

Octavia watched the comforting plump back of her sister leaving the room. How lucky she was to have May. Why did she find it so hard to show love to those she cared for?

***

So this was Nancarrow, thought Verity. She remembered all that Kitty had told her about the house and could see at once it must have been a beautiful home with views from the windows looking down the stepped garden of terraces to the lake below. It had an air of tranquillity and peace and she found it hard to believe that the family who had lived there had suffered so many tragedies. On being shown around by Octavia, Verity saw the rooms were high, light and airy, subdivided into wards of two and four beds. Old heavy coloured wallpaper had been stripped and the walls painted in restful pastel colours. The staff were kind and efficient and particularly patient with Kitty who because of her fluctuating and occasionally violent moods with additional problems in social and cognitive skills, was placed in a room on her own.

A nurse told them that Kitty was in the old library sitting in the armchair by the full length window and said the view of the fountain and the rose garden seemed to calm her. Verity wondered how Kitty would respond to seeing her after the month that had elapsed since her return to Cornwall. On leaving London, Kitty was thin, her strawberry blond hair lank around her face which still held the semblance of swelling and bruising. She was relieved now to see a little colour was back in her cheeks and with her leg and arm out of plaster, she was looking more like the Kitty she remembered. It was her eyes that brought home to Verity again the continuing seriousness of her condition. They were still dull and lifeless where once they danced with life and saw beyond the common place, but there was a spark of recognition accompanied by a vague smile.

'You've come,' she said haltingly.

'Yes. I'm so pleased to see you again Kitty. She kissed her.

'You have a lovely view of the rose garden.'

Kitty pointed towards the woods beyond. 'Swing on rope.'

Verity nodded. 'Yes, your mum said you liked to play on it when you were a little girl….'

'With Terry.'

'That's right, Kitty,' Octavia said. 'Did the nurse come today and help you to dress? She told me you're getting better at it now. Buttons are not easy are they?'

'Noooo. Hard.'

'Have you been for a walk in the garden yet?' Verity asked.

Kitty brooded on the question. 'I think so.'

'We went down to the lake together Kitty, didn't we?' Octavia prompted her. 'We sat on the seat overlooking the lake. It's very peaceful there with the sound of the water rushing down the weir into the lake and all the bird song,' Octavia explained to Verity.

There was the rattle of a trolley and an ancillary nurse entered the room with cups of tea and cakes. She clipped a tray across the chair and handed the cup to Kitty, who held it awkwardly, tipping the tea to one side where it fell and splashed up onto her blouse. With a low growling howl she pushed the cup over the tray onto the floor, gesticulating wildly with her hands.

'Kitty, Kitty,' Octavia said, attempting to stay her hands, but finding it impossible. Her strength surprised her and she grasped instantly the warning there of what could lie ahead once Kitty was home.

'I think it will probably be best if you could leave now,' the nurse said kindly. 'I will fetch another nurse and we'll settle her down. I'm afraid we get this quite often Mrs. Pengelly. It's frustration.'

With the nurse gone, Octavia tried again to hold Kitty's hands over the howls of temper. 'Kitty, listen... listen.... We have to go now. I will see you tomorrow.'

But Kitty was lost in her own world of confusion and darkness.

As they walked up the hill Octavia said, 'You can see how difficult it is. I think it's going to be a long time before Kitty is anywhere near to coming home.'

Verity agreed. 'It's very upsetting to see her like that, and distressing for Kitty too. She was bright and intelligent and I think on some very deep level she understands she's not right and doesn't know how to deal with it. It's an awful situation for you and your family Octavia. I'm so very sorry.'

'Yes, it's not easy. As a family we are all pulling together. Thomas will be home for the holidays, and Grace comes over from Falmouth as often as she can to see her. Kitty remembers us which is one blessing, but as for her marriage to Lawrence and having Amy, there's no memory at all,' she said, unhappily. They walked along the short terrace of houses and up the side entry to the back door of Octavia's home that had withstood and safeguarded her from the storms without and within its enduring granite walls.

'Friends to the back door, tradesmen at the front,' she joked, 'so you must do the same when you come next time.'

Verity smiled. 'Back door it is.'

Once inside, Octavia took Verity's collarless box jacket in navy linen over her matching dress and hung it on the hallstand, thinking to herself that Verity had style. She suggested they went into the front room to the armchairs in the bay window.

'We always sit here in the summer months. The room catches the afternoon and evening sun and the sunsets

139

are glorious out towards St. Michael's Mount. I'll just put the kettle on for tea. You'd better like saffron cake!' she quipped and Verity chuckled.

She was finding Octavia's humour typified the Cornish. She looked out from the window down the field from the terrace to the trees hiding Nancarrow. It was easy to imagine Kitty and Terry as two children playing in the grounds and stealing into the old deserted manor house. Her eyes travelled around the room at the decorative plasterwork ceilings, the white Sienna marble fireplace, the fine elaborate architrave of the door, and the deep step-cut skirting.

'This is a beautiful room, Octavia,' Verity remarked, when Octavia returned with a tray of tea and saffron cake.

'Yes it is. It's a very elegant house for a man who was once a poor miner. We were told he made his money in the gold fields of South Africa in the eighteen hundreds and had enough sense to hang onto it, return home and build this house. Not many did. It disappeared into the beer tents, gambling dens and brothels!' She put the tray down on the occasional table and cut a slice of saffron for Verity, who declared how she liked all Cornish fare and especially pasties!

Octavia smiled. 'Yes, most do. The children used to call me the pasty queen, as I make so many!'

'I'm not surprised they did. They're delicious! Your pastry is so soft,' Verity enthused.

'I'm glad you enjoyed it. It's a nice clean, easy meal, no washing up of pots and pans and the advantage of them is that they can be eaten hot or cold anywhere.' On finishing her piece of cake, Octavia said, 'On your next visit I shall make sure that May's here with Amy.'

Verity smiled with pleasure. 'I would so like to see Amy again and to meet May.'

'You'll probably see a change in Amy. She's growing away so fast. She reminds me very much of Kitty at her age, except she has a more placid nature. Kitty turned out to be a real tomboy and quite a handful. Thankfully, I don't think her daughter will take after her!'

The following week Verity found May installed in the kitchen making sandwiches for tea on their return from Nancarrow. Amy stood beside her on a kitchen chair, her doll swinging from her hand.

'I feel you two need very little introduction,' said Octavia, when May left the table and impulsively gave Verity a hug.

'At last we meet. I've heard so much about you.'

'And I you,' Verity laughed.

Octavia lifted Amy into her arms from the chair, her face alight with the happiness of holding her. 'Do you remember this lady Amy? She looked after you and brought you home with mummy?'

'Hello Amy. I see you're helping Aunty May to make sandwiches.'

Amy gave Verity a shy smile and nodded.

'And Granny's got a surprise for you Amy,' said Octavia. 'Would you like to see it?

Amy's round blue eyes looked at her in expectation from under a cloud of wispy fair hair.

'It's a cot where you can put your dolly to sleep. Your mummy used to play with it when she was a little girl. I remembered it was up in the loft May. Shall we go and find it, Amy?' Octavia said, carrying her out into the hall passage.

'You're so like your mummy,' they heard her say.

Verity and May exchanged glances of sympathetic commiseration at her words, and Verity could see why Kitty had spoken with such affection for her aunt. Her nature was warm and her hazel eyes registered friendly interest on meeting her. It had been the most enjoyable afternoon seeing the two sisters together and little Amy again. Octavia was right. She was growing like a fern, thought Verity on her way home on the train. If only she could confide in May about Kitty's half-sister Madeline, but it was out of the question. It was indeed a tangled web of relationships and secrets into which she had fallen.

Chapter Thirteen

OCTAVIA MADE HER way to the old library of Nancarrow with a daily sense of relief that her fears for Kitty staying there proved to be unfounded. It seemed whatever terror Kitty had experienced on that one occasion of them breaking in was not going to happen again. Kitty was sitting as usual in her favourite spot looking out through the elegant full-length windows and absorbed in watching the fountain spraying rainbow droplets. On her last visit she had taken her around the rose garden with its niches of Roman statues, and they'd wandered along the path to the mock remains of a Roman courtyard and sat beneath the shade of a trelliswork of roses. It had been a restful and pleasant afternoon for Kitty had been in a state of calm.

'Hello Kitty,' she said quietly. How are you feeling?' she asked, sitting down beside her. She glanced at the gathering dark clouds threatening to hide the sun. 'I don't think it would be wise to go into the garden today, it's beginning to look like rain.'

'N-e-v-e-r mind, mummy' Kitty replied. Her speech was halting.

'Yes, we can go outside another day.' Octavia opened her handbag. 'Kitty, I want to show you something.' She handed her a photo of Amy. 'Do you know who this is?'

Kitty stared vacantly at the photo of Amy.

'Nooo.'

'It's your little daughter Amy.' Octavia could see it meant nothing.

'Where's Grace?

'Grace will be here on Sunday,' and thinking it would help Kitty's memory to reinforce the change in family circumstances said, 'Chris, her husband, will be bringing her over in the car from Falmouth. That's where Grace lives now since they were married.'

'Grace is married.'

'Yes, that's right.'

'Will Thomas come?'

'In the school holidays, he will. He's a teacher now in Bristol which is a long way away.'

'Yoooo love him best.'

Given Kitty's state of confusion, Octavia was taken aback at this remembered assumption from childhood, although she grudgingly admitted to herself, it did have an element of truth. Her love for Thomas had been defensive, a son she had waited for, and, unlike her eldest tomboy of a daughter, was placid and malleable to her will. Grace, shy and quiet, played her own game with a willpower that could stubbornly defy all reason.

'That's not true, Kitty. I love you all,' she said firmly.'

'Noooo, you don't!' she said, slowly and vehemently.

'I want to see Terry. Why d-o-e-s-n-'t he come?' she asked petulantly.

It was something Octavia had come to expect, this random switching of subject.

Octavia hesitated. This was awkward. How much did Kitty remember? How far back should she go? She decided to play safe with Kitty's last memory of him. 'Terry went away to be apprenticed as a cabinetmaker in Exeter. That's why he can't be here.'

Octavia could see Kitty was puzzled at this.

'I don't r-e-m-e-m-b-e-r.'

'Don't worry. Your memory will get better as time goes on.'

'When can I see M-a-d-e-l-i-n-e? I want to see her.'

'You've asked me about her before Kitty. I don't know who you mean.'

'She's my sister!'

'You only have one sister Kitty, and that's Grace.'

Kitty became agitated. 'No! M-a-d-e-l-i-n-e. My sister, too.'

Who on earth was this Madeline that Kitty was constantly referring to? To distract her, Octavia took from her handbag a bag of jelly babies.

'Look Kitty, I've brought your favourite sweets.'

Kitty smacked her hand away. 'Don't want them!'

With a sinking certainty Octavia realized this was how it was going to be for months, if not years to come. Kitty locked in the memory of a young child. After the initial relief and happiness at seeing Kitty on her return from Malaysia, she was now overcome at the enormity of the problems ahead. She needed help in dressing, in using the bathroom, and was clumsy with anything requiring dexterity. In frustration she lashed out with unintelligible words and fought the nurse's attempts to give her medication. Her recovery was more challenging than she had ever imagined.

***

Verity pushed Robert in his pram down through the Morrab gardens where the gardeners were busy turning over the summer beds in preparation for winter, and out onto the promenade. The weather had rounded on them with a foretaste of winter; the sky lit with sulphurous shafts of light over a sullen rolling sea and she hurried along the pavement to her cottage, spurred on with the thought of a warming cup of tea. Nowhere on this planet did the weather change as rapidly and round-about-face as in Cornwall she thought, opening her door and parking the pram in the small entrance lobby. She lifted Robert out and placing him in the small baby pen that Terry had fashioned for her use, went into the kitchen and returned with saucepans and lids for Robert to play with, having latterly discovered to her amusement, they were far more interesting and noisy than the toys she kept in the cottage for his visits. She clucked lovingly at him and dropping them into his pen, returned to the kitchen and switched the kettle on, her thoughts troubled as she recalled her last meeting with Octavia and the minefield presented to her out of the blue when chatting about Kitty's progress.

'I don't suppose you know of anyone Kitty knew who was called Madeline?' Octavia asked her. 'She keeps repeating her name and saying she's her sister of all things! And she wants to see her and Terry the boy she grew up with next door.'

Octavia's eyes intent on cutting slices of her homemade Victorian sponge missed Verity's alarmed reaction to her question.

'I've been wondering whether to ask Mrs. Retallack if it would be possible for Terry to come and visit Kitty,' she went on. 'It's all a bit awkward really as there was a time when he and Kitty were engaged and I understand he has recently married and is now living in Penzance. Anyway, she seems to have fastened onto the name of Madeline like a dog with a bone.'

Octavia handed her a slice of the sponge, and pouring the tea said, 'I don't know of anyone from her childhood called this name. I wondered if it was one of the nurses, but it seems not. Could it be a friend of hers from Malaysia, do you think?'

Verity composed her features, hardly knowing how to answer her.

'No. I don't think so. She has never spoken about anyone of that name to me. I wouldn't put too much store by it. Kitty's mind is still pretty jumbled at the moment. Perhaps Thomas or Grace may know of someone; talking of which. How is Thomas getting on in Bristol?' she asked, in desperation to lead Octavia away to another topic.

'Oh, he's settling down very well into teaching and likes Bristol and the area very much.'

But Octavia's train of thought was still on Madeline and to Verity's dismay she returned to it.

'I'm pretty sure neither Thomas nor Grace have ever mentioned the name, but if it is someone in Malaysia, it's the first sign we've had that Kitty remembers her life out there, and that would be real progress,' said Octavia with hope in her voice.

Verity agreed and pointedly glanced at her watch, anxious to be away despite the fact it would mean her having to wait at the station for the best part of an hour. She could not remain sitting any longer and having to lie in Octavia's pursuit for an answer. She hastily finished her cake.

'That was 'ansum,' she said in light-hearted banter to cover her disquiet.

'Verity, we'll make a Cornishman of you yet!' Octavia smiled. 'Would you like another piece?'

'Thank you, but no. I really must be making a move. I'm meeting some friends tonight for a rubber of bridge so I'm catching the earlier train.' She felt her cheeks redden with the falsehood.

'Of course, I'll just get your coat from the hall. It's a good game, bridge. I played it in the dim and distant past before children came along.'

Verity racked with guilt stood up. 'Thank you so much my dear as always for my pasty lunch and welcome cup of tea. I know I come to see Kitty, but I also do look forward to our time together,' she said on Octavia's return.

'Yes, and I feel the same,' agreed Octavia. 'Out of bad has come good; our friendship. Oh, I haven't told you have I,' she went on, helping Verity into her coat, 'there's talk that Kitty will be able to come home well before Christmas as she is suddenly beginning to make strides in looking after herself and is taking an interest in Amy. Of course, Christmas is a long way off yet, but already I'm planning for everyone to be here on Christmas Day.

'That's wonderful news Octavia. For Kitty to have all her family around her at such a time will do her a power of good and hopefully stir a few more memories.'

'Yes, that would be the icing on the cake for us. I would love for you to join us if you haven't any other plans. With the scant public transport over Christmas you'd be welcome to stop overnight.'

'As it happens, I've already made tentative arrangements to be with friends in Penzance over Christmas, but thank you so much for the thought.'

'In that case, you'll have to come up and share a pre-Christmas drink with us all.'

'That would be simply lovely, Octavia. I shall look forward to it.'

***

Verity stepped up into her living room and sat watching Robert chewing on the knob of the sauce pan lid and thinking how strange the workings of the mind that Kitty should recollect the name of Madeline and yet not know her own baby daughter. She picked Robert up, bouncing him up and down on one knee to the rhyme of

'Ride a cock horse,' speeding up at the end to hear his chuckling laughter and she laughed along with him. How she loved this baby who filled her day with happiness. She drew him close to her, thinking of her next meeting with Octavia. She made up her mind. There was no way around it, Octavia must be told about James and Madeline. She would reap the whirlwind, and most upsetting of all Octavia would know of her deception in a friendship that was knitted together by their love of Kitty. She hardly dared to think about it.

She sat Robert in his pram and tucked the blankets around him. 'Time to take you home my little man. If only we could stay as young and innocent as you, what a wonderful place the world would be.'

Chapter Fourteen

TERRY STOOD UP from his work desk stretched and walked over to the turret window. The room was stuffy and he opened the window and felt the rush of soft air on his face. He gazed out at the glittering sea thinking how ideal the turret room must have been for a captain of a ship, albeit a rather nefarious one. A late fishing smack was making its way out of Newlyn and far out on the horizon he could see the black smudge of a tanker. With not a cloud in the sky, it was a day to be outside and to enjoy, and turning thought into action he clattered down the narrow turret steps along the corridor past the bedroom doors and down into the kitchen.

Madeline's head was deep in the oven's interior.

'I've decided we should go out for the day! Make the most of this beautiful weather,' he enthused, as he put the kettle on to make coffee. 'It's nearly the end of September. We won't get many more days like this.'

A dishevelled Madeline emerged. 'What?'

'I said, let's go out for the day once Robert is awake from his morning nap.'

'Terry! I'm right in the middle of cleaning the oven, as you can see, and I'm a mess.'

'You can finish it tomorrow.'

Madeline sighed and sat back on her heels. 'Typical man! And what about your work?'

'It won't run away. This day is too good to waste. I'll ring Colin to let him know I'm not around and then boil the eggs for sandwiches, sort out some fruit that could do with eating, and make a flask of tea—

'Not to mention the business of getting together the paraphernalia needed for Robert.'

'I can do that whilst you're seeing to Robert and yourself.'

'I'm not going to get out of this, am I?' Madeline surrendered with a grin. 'Where were you thinking of going?'

'Somewhere you said you hadn't been to before. Porthcurnow. I thought we could take in the Minack Theatre at the same time.'

Madeline's eyes brightened at the thought. 'I've always wanted to see it but when working and having no car—'

'Well there you are then. Have van will travel. So what are you waiting for?' His blue eyes were teasing. 'Come on, jump to it woman! Chop! Chop!'

After a flurry of activity, Terry stowed the picnic blanket, food and Robert's bag inside the van. He attached to the floor a child's high chair he had adapted to sit behind them between the seats, and with a dazed Robert rapidly fed, watered, changed and strapped into the chair, they set off.

Madeline had to grant Terry it was a lovely day and was glad he had overridden her protests as they bowled along the country road towards Land's End. She cast him a sideways look. She was still amazed by him; his patience, his sense of fun, his love for her, and his artistry in furniture making. She was inordinately proud of him and smiled to herself from sheer happiness. London seemed another world and was. Nothing could compare to this beautiful county that she fell in love with as a child and was drawn back to by its magic and a love that waited.

Terry glanced at her and caught Madeline's secret smile.

'Happy darling?'

'Blissfully! I'm almost purring!'

Terry's face creased in amusement.

'I love you and our baby so much Terry. I couldn't bear it if anything happened to take this happiness away.' Her eyes became anxious. 'You won't ever leave me, will you?'

'Of course I won't. Whatever makes you think that? You know how much I love you.'

He reached for her hand and kissed it before turning off from the Land's End road to Porthcurnow on the long valley road to the cove where they parked, and unloading the pushchair and bags they walked along the sandy path to emerge above the beach. A sea of Mediterranean blue gently lapped the shelving white sand where sheltering cliffs rose to each side from rocks to dense green vegetation.

Madeline gave a gasp. 'It's stunning!'

'It is rather special, isn't it? Hard to believe messages have whizzed around the world from here in cables hidden beneath the sand. It was like a fortress in the war. And wait until you see the theatre. It's spectacular. We'll drive up to it and take a look when we leave for home. Glad you've come now?'

'Let's just say cleaning an oven doesn't compare to this!'

The beach was theirs for the taking with only a sprinkling of people for it was off the beaten track and the week-end trippers were gone. They spread themselves out luxuriating in the heat of an Indian summer, squinting at its dazzling light off the water. Robert crawled to the edge of the blanket and picking up a handful of sand pushed it into his mouth.

'Why does everything dirty have to go straight to their mouths?' Madeline cried, snatching him up and attempting to brush the sand from his face with her hand.

'Especially my slippers! They're very tasty!' Terry agreed with a grin. 'I think you'll need this,' he said, opening a bottle of water and wetting a corner of the towel.

Robert protested against the invasion in and around his mouth, pushing her hands away and twisting and turning his head.

'It's like trying to hold a squirming eel,' Madeline said. He arched his back to be set down and like a wound-up toy took off a speed across the blanket.

'Come here you little monkey!' she laughed. He chuckled at her hauling him back and immediately rolled over onto his belly to do it all over again.

'Oh no, you don't!' Madeline said, sitting him between her legs. 'I think we'd better put him in his push chair Terry or we shall spend the rest of the afternoon chasing after him.'

Terry scooped him up into his arms. 'I've got a better idea. Right my little tearaway,' he said, nuzzling into his neck and blowing raspberries that brought forth a paroxysm of chuckles, 'are you coming for a swim with daddy? I'll take him down to the sea and dip his toes. He won't be expecting the shock of cold water!' He looked down at Madeline, who slim and unmarked by childbirth stretched herself out on a towel in a trendy pink denim bikini. The sun highlighted the copper glints in her blond hair. She was as lovely as any model fronting a magazine. He was a fortunate man when fate stepped in and shown him that life with Madeline could be sweeter and finer that he had ever imagined.

Madeline watched Terry carrying Robert to the sea, his figure lean and muscled from cutting and working in wood. Her eyes were soft with the depth of her love for him and then she shivered from a sudden cold dart down her body. Someone's just walked over my grave, and she instantly thought of Kitty, the girl who had lived next door to Terry; her doppelganger. Despite the fact she had accepted Terry's casual explanation that Kitty was a childhood friend, she seemed to resurface in her mind whenever she was at her happiest.

Terry held Robert's sturdy little chest and body and dipped his toes in and out of the bubbling water's edge. Robert drew his knees up and Terry looked back at Madeline laughing and signalled for her to join them. She pushed herself to her feet and waving back walked across the shell-strewn sand to the sea, telling herself she was being ridiculous to worry about someone she didn't even know and who lived an ocean away. The cove's bewitching beauty under a hot periwinkle blue sky was Pantheistic and she felt its magic caressing her body and lifting her spirits. A white feather drifted down in front of her and settled at her feet. She picked it up and looked up at the cloudless sky. There was not a bird in sight, or even the cry of a gull at sea. She had heard of angel's calling cards, feathers that appeared from nowhere, symbolizing their love and protection. She had been sent a sign. Her fears were groundless. The promise was in her hand and placing the feather in the cleft of a rock to retrieve on her return, she continued to the two people waiting who she loved more than life itself.

Later, with Robert nodding into sleep in his shaded push chair, tranquillized with the sun and his bottle of milk, they sat in quiet contentment, gazing at the fringe of ruffled water inching up the sand from a sparkling sea. It seemed impossible to believe winter would come bringing long grey days and driving drizzle that penetrated the bones, and winds raging in from a stormy Atlantic that could lift them off their feet.

Terry draped his arm around her shoulders holding her close and their kiss was long and deep.

'I'm glad you brought me here,' she murmured. 'St. Ives will always be my favourite, but this is magical and so peaceful *"far from the madding crowd."* Hardy's words sum it up perfectly.' She nestled into his shoulder. 'I don't think I've ever told you this before but a strange thing happened to me at St. Ives when I was about six or seven. I've never forgotten it. I was standing with mum and Aunt Verity on the station waiting to go home when I saw identical twins; two little girls who looked the spitting image of me, the same strawberry blond hair, everything. I couldn't believe my eyes. One of them seemed to glow like sunshine and when we reached St. Erth station to change trains, she vanished into thin air amongst the crowd waiting for the Camborne Redruth train on the other side of the track.'

Madeline paused, reflecting on it.

'I believe now she was a ghost because she was so still and quiet. I remember thinking on the train going home that the sunshine twin reminded me of a lady who was killed during the war. I saw her after a bomb destroyed her house and both she and the twin had the same shining aura. The other twin was very much alive, playing with the beads on her sister's chair and making her laugh by tickling her under the chin. I always hoped to see the twins again but I never did.

As Madeline related the incident, Terry's blood turned cold. Madeline had seen Kitty as a child and the ghost of her identical twin sister who died at birth. The sister in the pushchair was clearly Grace, before Thomas was born. He could hardly believe the coincidence of her seeing them and brought flashbacks

155

of growing up with Kitty; the flowering of their childhood love that grew with the years, and where marriage was accepted as the natural outcome until she met Lawrence and their plans for a life together were extinguished.

Madeline felt his body stiffen and she turned from her gaze at the sea to Terry and was shocked at his pallor.

'You're looking awfully pale. Are you alright?'

Terry's mouth went dry. He could keep it from her no longer.

'There's something I must tell you.'

The seriousness of his expression alarmed her and she sat back from him with a feeling of apprehension.

'What's the matter? Has something happened to the business?'

'No, nothing like that. It's.......it's about Kitty, the girl who used to live next door to me. You asked me once about her.'

Madeline's heart began to thud. Here it was at last, the answer to the name that haunted her.

'We did grow up together but what I didn't admit was that we were engaged to be married, until she met someone else and broke it off.'

'I *knew* it,' she half-whispered. 'I *knew* there was something special about her. It was the way you reacted when you first saw me, and called out her name. I tried to ignore it but all the time I had this feeling you weren't completely mine.'

'No! That's not true Maddy. I loved you from the moment I saw you. You know that.'

'Do I?' Her voice rose. 'Do I really? I think you love me because I look like her. But how can we look so alike, unless....' She stopped, seized with a shock of understanding as she remembered the fateful day her Faith confessed to her affair with James, a married man she met in Malaysia and by whom she'd had Madeline, and there was no mistaking Terry's first startled reaction in thinking she was Kitty.

'She's my sister, isn't she? My God! You were in love with my sister!'

'Yes, I was,' wholly stricken that he had had to admit it to her.

Madeline felt her world disintegrating. She was paralysed with the fear of it. 'I can't bear it.' Tears rolled down her shocked face.

Terry folded his arms around her.'

'Maddy please don't cry. I love you so very much and I've never been happier than with you and our beautiful son. You must believe me.'

She did not move within his arms, but sat as stone, her face wet with tears.

'Maddy look at me.'

He drew her face to him. The sadness in her eyes tore him apart. He had to convince Kitty of the depth of his love for her.

'Darling, my love for Kitty died a long time ago. I admit you do bear a resemblance to Kitty and it seems you both have the gift of second sight, but in character you're very different. When I first met you, you were so funny and beautiful babbling on about storms and ghosts. I knew I'd found someone I wanted to spend the rest of my life with. You are the best part of me. We fit together. You know we do. We have the same expectations, the same outlook on life. Kitty was a tomboy, constantly looking for excitement which was fine when we were children, but when we grew up and became engaged, I think subconsciously I always suspected she wanted something different from life, and she found it in Lawrence, the man she married.'

'But why didn't you tell me all this when I asked about her?'—

'Because we were just married and I didn't want to give you any reason to doubt my love.'

She shook her head miserably. 'I still don't understand. How could you have known that Kitty was my half-sister, apart from the fact you say I look like her?'

His stomach twisted into a knot. By revealing everything he was running the risk of losing her.

'When Kitty came home for her father's funeral and to have her baby, she said she had discovered from Verity that she had a half-sister called Madeline.'

'*Verity?*! Verity knows my *sister*?! Madeline shook her head in disbelief. 'How and why has she never told me?' she asked, cut to the quick that Verity could have kept such a monumental secret from her.

'Because I asked her not to. You see when Verity and I first met at our wedding we couldn't believe the coincidence of us knowing both you and Kitty. She asked me if you knew you had a half-sister and that we'd been engaged to be married. I admitted I hadn't told you yet and she said the sooner I did the better because someone might let it slip. I agreed and said I would when I felt the time was right. Since then she has kept my confidence, something I know she's not found easy.'

'So that was what you and Verity were discussing in the garden when I came out and you pretended everything was hunky-dory between you. How clever you two are at keeping secrets,' I snapped.

Terry flinched. 'I couldn't bear for anything to upset you before our wedding, Maddy, you must believe that. Verity met Kitty in the dining room of the hotel in Malaysia and mistakenly thought Kitty was you. She and her husband Lawrence, a mining engineer, were in transit up to Northern Perak. They quickly became friends and Kitty invited her to come and stay on the mine. It was then Kitty discovered she had a half-sister in you when looking through some family photos. Verity recognized your father as the man Faith had an affair with, and not only that, Maurice knew him as well because he fought with your father behind enemy lines in Malaysia where he was killed. And there's something else you should know,' anxious that everything should now be said. 'Kitty sees things from the past. In one of her time-slips she saw your father James with Faith on the dance floor of the hotel in Malaysia. She was always very psychic, even as a child,' he said, thinking of the ghosts of Nancarrow.

Madeline's face was one of incredulity. 'I don't know what to say. It's all so bizarre, it's beyond belief.'

'Kitty used to say there's no such thing as coincidences, life was mapped out. She seems to have been proved uncannily right.' His eyes dropped at Madeline's stiff stare.

'Please believe me, darling. I really did intend to tell you all this a lot sooner, but then you became pregnant with Robert and there never seemed to be a good time. I did talk the whole thing over with my parents'—

'You told them as well?'

'I had to because of your resemblance to Kitty. They couldn't miss it. They'd known Kitty all her life and it's why they behaved a little strangely to you. It was inconceivable to them that I should meet and marry her sister! Not only that, Kitty's mother Octavia is still living next door, putting them into the very awkward situation of now knowing her husband James had an affair that resulted in you. So you can see their dilemma and mine.'

'No, I don't see,' she retorted, her tears turning to anger. 'All I see is that everybody has kept something from me I had a right to know. First Faith, and now I find you grew up with my half-sister, and as if that wasn't enough, you were in love with her! I've been living in cloud cuckoo land. I feel such a fool,' she said, bitterly.

'Maddy, you know—

A thought struck her. 'And what if Kitty decided to contact me through Verity? What would you have done then?'

'Actually, she did want to meet you but felt it would be disloyal to her mother who knew nothing about James's affair and as far as I know, still doesn't.'

'Well, that makes two of us kept in the dark like mushrooms!'

Robert stirred, opening his eyes and mewing like a bird. 'He needs a drink,' Madeline said, sharply.

Terry rummaged around in the baby bag and took out a bottle of rosehip syrup. 'After this, shall I give him the jar of rice pudding?'

She jumped to her feet. 'Work it out for yourself. I'm going for a walk and try and make sense of everything. If that's possible! And Robert will probably need changing,' she threw back at him as she walked away.

He lifted Robert out of his pushchair, sat him on his lap and gave him the drink.

'I think your Mummy's angry with me and she has every right to be,' he said straining his head around Robert to see where Madeline was going. He saw she was making her way from the beach to the path when she disappeared from view.

With her thoughts in turmoil, and barely aware of where she was going, she headed up the steep hill to the open air theatre built into the cliffs. His words spun around in her head. She was confused and angry and most of all felt betrayed by those that professed to love her. Her thoughts went back to Stuart in London keeping from her the salient fact that he already had a wife. How easy men found it to compartmentalize their lives, she fumed; keeping their family secrets in little boxes as if they were of no consequence or concern to anyone else and even Faith had kept hidden the secret of her birth. God! What a mess people make of their lives. And now this shock of discovering Terry had loved her half-sister, enough to marry her. It rocked her faith in him as nothing else could. Her eyes smarted at the thought. She blinked away the tears and speeded up her steps, concentrating instead on the physicality of negotiating the steep gradient which left her panting on the cliff top.

She stood looking down on the cove. The translucent turquoise sea sparkled like a tropical jewel against the white sand now turning to gold in the late afternoon sun dropping to meet the sea. She could just make out Robert sitting in his pushchair and Terry spooning rice into his eager little mouth. Her heart stopped at the sight, and she stepped back quickly before Terry should look up and see her. She walked along to the theatre hidden from view beneath the cliffs, and gave a little gasp. Terry was right. It was spectacular.

In front of her lay a Greek amphitheatre, designed and shaped into the cliffs by Rowena Cade; a lady with a vision to bring the arts to the people. With the help of her gardener over a lifetime of backbreaking work moving rocks and earth, they had made a theatre with stone columns and arches and small balconies set into the rocks. Grass topped seats fell steeply in steps to a paving stone stage with a raised two step dais in the centre and away to the corner. Beyond was the backdrop of the sea of Porthcurnow bay, like a whispering sprite in her ears, and on its rocky promontory lay the famous rocking Logan rock.

The last lingering visitors were leaving and she had the theatre to herself. She sat on one of the grass seats, soaking up its unique atmosphere. It seemed to quieten her racing heart and battered feelings, took her away to another time and place. What a setting for Shakespeare's *The Tempest* on a wild night, she mused, with the moaning wind tossing the sea and whipping it high to drench the performers as it was known to do on a stormy evening performance. She closed her eyes, sensing the ghosts of thespians past. She reflected on the golden age of Athens, the great statesmen and orators in an assembly of men laying the foundations for democracy and searching for the meaning of life in surroundings such as this.

Immersed in her thoughts, her pain and anger began to melt away with a sudden sea mist that swirled around her. Time ceased to exist. She could feel every particle of her connected to creation, to that which had gone before and that which was to come. Life and death were as one and love was at its centre. A divine sense of peace washed over her at this teaching, and as suddenly as the mist appeared, it parted and drifted out over the sea into a cloudless sky, taking with it the wisdom of the ancients.

She was roused from her dream-like state by the cry of a sea bird and she wondered how long she had been sitting there. Terry would be wondering where she was and with a sense of urgency she left the theatre and hurried to the beach, half running in her eagerness down the hill to those she loved. Terry was laughing and playing with Robert on the sand. The sight brought tears to her eyes and she quickly brushed them away. He must not think her tears were still of reproach. Terry turned and saw her, his eyes lighting up and then becoming uncertain. Madeline smiled and lifting her arms around his neck, held his loving blue eyes with hers with all the love she could express in a touch and look.

'I love you. Let's forget about the past,' she murmured, 'and let's go home. It's been quite a day,' and then she remembered the feather. 'Oh, I nearly forgot. There's something I must retrieve from the rocks before we go.'

Terry looked at her bemused.

'You'll see in a minute,' she laughed, and made her way to the rocks and on her return waved the feather under his nose.

'It's an angel's calling card,' she began to explain when Terry interrupted.

'Not you too!' and then stopped with a look of guilt.

'What do you mean, not you too?'

'Well, it's just that Kitty told me about an angel's feather she brought home from this beach when she was a little girl. I'm sorry darling. I didn't mean to bring Kitty into our conversation again.'

'I know and it's OK. She was a part of your life. Stuart was a part of mine. We can't act as if they never existed. Our past shapes us to become who we are.'

'Oh Maddy, I love you so much,' he said, pulling her close.

Robert, sitting on the blanket, looked up at them both and seizing his opportunity made off like a rocket.

They both laughed as Madeline went after him. Terry began to pack up their beaching gear.

'Let's take our tearaway home!' he said, with a smile of such happiness it melted her bones.

Chapter Fifteen

VERITY HAD NEVER seen Madeline in such a state of nervous excitement, her face flushed with the exertion of pushing the pram against a wind that had blown away the heat of yesterday's sun and was slicing across the prom.

'Oh Verity I'm so glad I've found you in! I was going to ring but then I thought I had to see you. It was too important to talk about over a phone.'

'You're sounding very mysterious,' Verity replied, helping Madeline in with Robert's pram. I'll let you sort out the playpen for Robert in the kitchen whilst I put the kettle on.'

Madeline hastily pulled open the playpen, sat Robert inside and picking up an armful of soft toys from Verity's toy box, and the old saucepan and lid to bang together, she dropped them in and hovered around Verity like a bee who taking a tin of biscuits from the cupboard began to make the tea.

'Madeline for heaven's sake sit down, you're like a cat with its tail on fire!' and was taken back to a memory of Madeline as a little girl getting under her feet in the kitchen.

Madeline couldn't help but smile at her remark. From childhood Verity remained a second mother to her, and right then, acted and sounded exactly like one.

Madeline did as she was told. 'Sorry. It's just so much has happened in the last twenty four hours, I don't know if I'm on my head or my heels.'

Verity seating herself opposite, pushed a mug of tea across the table with a crooked smile. 'Well, maid, what are 'ee so worked up about? Let's be hearen it!'

Madeline snorted with laughter. 'Oh Verity! You'll never get the lingo. You're much too posh.'

'I try!'

'Seriously though, the news is that yesterday Terry dropped the bombshell on me that I have a half-sister called Kitty.'

'Ah! So Terry has finally taken the bull by the horns,' Verity replied with relief.

'He also said you know her but he'd made you promise not to tell me.' She frowned. 'He had no right to do that.'

'I admit I certainly wasn't happy about it.'

'I've never told you this, but I asked Terry once about Kitty because when I met him, he mistook me for her and called me her name. It always bothered me. His reply was that I looked like a girl who used to live next door to him. What he didn't admit to was being in love with her and they were engaged to be married.'

Verity sighed. 'There was his opportunity to tell you, and he should have done so then.'

'Well, I certainly know now! I've tossed and turned on it all night wondering what she's like. I feel I can't talk to Terry, they've been too close for comfort, so I've only you to ask. Both you and Terry have mistaken us for one another, so we must look awfully alike. Are we? You will tell me, won't you?' she asked hesitantly at the look of disquiet on Verity's face.

'Yes, of course I will. I must say I think you're taking it all remarkably well.'

'Believe me, I didn't at first. In fact, I was so angry I left him with Robert on Porthcurnow beach where we'd gone for the day, and stormed away and ended up at the Minack. I've never seen the theatre before and whilst there I had the most magical experience, which I must tell you about later, and it made me realize the only thing that mattered was my love for Terry, not what happened in our lives before we met. On the beach he couldn't have been more patient or loving when he explained about Kitty or made it clearer how much he loved me and Robert. Kitty is most definitely in the past!'

Verity nodded in agreement with a half-smile of understanding, but there was an underlying despondency in the cast of her face that worried Madeline.

'So, what *is* she like?'

'Well, you're very similar in many ways. You're both psychic for a start. Kitty sees people from past lives, and has done so since childhood, and unfortunately when she married Lawrence he had no patience with it. He put her staring into space episodes down to Petit Mal until proven otherwise by the doctor. Kitty had a lovely bubbly personality and was well liked with a generosity of spirit that included inviting the lonely bachelors, married and otherwise, for a meal in Malaysia. I met a few of them and they were good company especially when well oiled with drink. The anecdotes and yarns they told!' she said, smiling at the thought. 'There's no denying you resemble one another. You have the same build, the same colour hair, longish face with high cheek bones and a similar shaped mouth, but your nose is quite different and I've never seen anyone with eyes like hers. They are the most amazing colour of emerald green. I used to think they were otherworldly…,' she tailed off, as if about to say something more but thought better of it.

Madeline felt a prick of alarm. 'Verity why do I get the feeling you're not telling me everything and a couple of times you spoke of her in the past tense. She's not dead or dying is she?'

Verity flustered, 'No, no, she's alive but not too good right now. She was in a car accident in Malaysia and was flown back and is in a nursing home in Camborne.'

'Oh. No. Was she badly hurt? Terry never said anything to me about that.'

'I'm sure he doesn't know, or he would have told you.'

'But you do, so why didn't you tell him?'

'Actually, I was going to ask if I could see you both. The accident it's something I need to talk to you and Terry about together. What evening would be best to come up and see you?'

Madeline's reply was immediate. 'Come for supper tonight and you can tell us everything. From the look on your face I can see it's serious.'

'Yes it is, and decisions are going to have to be made.'

After Madeline's flurry of a visit to her cottage, Verity hastened that evening to Terry and Madeline and after their meal, she confessed to her weekly visits of seeing Kitty in Nancarrow following her catastrophic car accident. Keeping the details as unemotional as she could, she filled them in on her injuries and coma and her slow recovery and explained that Kitty's little girl was being looked after by Octavia and May. It was like a burden had fallen from her shoulders. It had not been easy concealing her weekly visits to Kitty and particularly difficult on one occasion when Madeline had, on the spur of the moment, rung and suggested them getting together that day, and caught on the hop, she had given a feeble excuse not to meet. Madeline had sounded piqued and there was not a thing she could have done about it.

167

Terry was horrified. 'Is there no hope of her recovery, of some sort of normality?'

'It could happen, but it's a long process,' Verity replied.

'But why didn't my parents or you tell me this before?'

'How could we? It would have been difficult under the circumstances, don't you think?' Verity replied, with an ironic raise of her eyebrows at him. 'Up until now Madeline had no idea she had a half-sister!'

'Yes, I have to admit I'm at fault there. Kitty was always so full of life. I can't stand to think of her in such an awful state.' He looked away, striving to control his emotions.

Madeline felt an irrational twinge of resentment at Terry's obvious distress. 'And her husband Lawrence what happened to him?' she asked.

'He was killed outright,' Verity replied.

'My God! What a heartache for his parents,' Madeline said, thinking she would rather die herself than lose Robert.

'But what was Mrs. Pengelly thinking of putting her in Nancarrow?' he demanded. 'Kitty hated the place.'

Verity quickly reassured him. 'Octavia didn't want her to go into Nancarrow either, it was the doctor's decision. There's no need to worry, Kitty's happy there and likes to sit in the old library looking out at the fountain and garden.'

'I remember it well,' said Terry, 'a wonderful old room with a full length heraldic window.'

'Yes, that's it. Anyway, the main reason I'm here this evening is because Kitty is asking to see you both.'

Terry and Madeline exchanged a look of astonishment.

'She has no memory of her life with Lawrence but somehow her muddled mind has retained the knowledge that she has a half-sister. Perhaps Madeline you were uppermost in her thoughts before the accident and because of this she remembers your name. The mind is a funny thing. I was put into a very difficult position when Octavia asked if I knew anyone called Madeline. I had to lie to her. So you see from my point of view, this situation cannot go on any longer. Octavia is going to have to be told about you, Madeline, and your father James.'

'Yes, I can see that,' Terry said, 'but I can't help wondering that once Mrs. Pengelly hears of James's affair, which is going to be quite a shock for her, whether she'll be willing for Madeline to see Kitty.' He paused, thinking. 'On the other hand, she was always down-to-earth and practical, and I think she will quickly realise if it helps Kitty to see us both, then it's something she will have to face and accept.' He sighed heavily. 'What a kettle of fish this is.'

'Yes, it's certainly that, and the sooner it's resolved the better and it looks like I'm going to have to be the one to tell her and I don't relish the thought!'

Chapter Sixteen

OCTAVIA SAT IN her small dusky-pink moquette armchair showing signs of wear from many years of usage, but one she could not bring herself to throw away for it held too many memories and remained in the big bay of her bedroom. She began slip-hemming a skirt, now unfashionably long, and busy with her needle, her mind went back to the war years and May sitting in the chair opposite following her shift at Holmans when her first thought on arriving home was always for Kitty. And here they were, once more, keeping watch with hope and prayers that she would return to full strength and normality. Her recovery had been painfully slow but with summer relaxing into the mellow days of autumn, they were beginning to see a glimmer of the Kitty they remembered. Her rehabilitation with intensive speech therapy was making inroads in her ability to communicate, and her skill in co-ordination of movement was advancing with physiotherapy. Her eyes were coming back to life and her words stumbled over themselves in the mammoth effort to speak coherently. Kitty was fighting back. She still did not remember Amy, although with the regular contact on seeing her with Octavia, a seed of attachment appeared to be taking root.

She thought about Verity's last phone call confirming their weekly arrangements and saying she would be arriving a little later as she had an appointment for a check-up at the dentist and hoped that would be alright. Verity had not sounded herself at all with a tremor in her voice that made Octavia feel strangely uneasy.

Something was amiss she felt sure. Her hands stilled for a moment and she stared out at the trees of Nancarrow which were beginning to shed their golden red leaves, and through which she could glimpse the thin blue line of the sea to the North Cliffs. Had Verity heard some troubling news of some sort, she wondered? In a short space of time she'd become very fond of her; drawn to her kindness and good manners and her quiet sense of humour that appreciated the nuances of Cornish wit. Such a sadness that she was unable to have children of her own, but then her thoughts ran on, in having children you have to face the chance of losing them in a split second of time with all the heartache that comes with it: her poor broken Kitty, struggling so hard to bring herself back into the world. She sighed softly and began to sing one of Kitty's favourite hymns under her breath, and on finishing the skirt, stood up and shook it out ready to iron.

***

Under her umbrella, Verity made her way slowly up the steep hill from the station to Octavia's house feeling as grey and dismal as the weather, which had, with typical Cornish perverseness turned from an early morning of cloudy blue skies to rain. Her thoughts were consumed with the difficult confession that lay ahead and apprehensive as to how Octavia would respond to the distressing news of James's extra marital affair with Faith, and she was deeply aware of her breach of trust in their new-found friendship. Verity knocked on the back door.

'Come in,' Octavia sang out.

'Hello, my dear,' Verity said as she came into the kitchen to find Octavia checking the pasties in the oven.

'Another ten minutes and they'll be ready,' smiled Octavia. 'What a miserable day,' she went on, looking keenly at Verity whose whole demeanour gave Octavia a foreboding in the pit of her stomach. Whatever it might be, a glass of sherry she often found smoothed the way.

'Shall we have a glass of sherry whilst we're waiting?'

'Yes, why not,' replied Verity, with similar sentiments running through her mind.

They moved into the sitting room where the table was laid, and watching Octavia pour them each a generous glass of sherry, Verity had the sudden mad urge to drink the whole bottle and pass into oblivion.

They sat and talked of books they had read and one that Verity had recently borrowed from the library, *The Prime of Miss Jean Brodie* which she had enjoyed and thought that Octavia would find a good read.

'I shall look out for it when I'm next in the library,' Octavia replied, 'and I think those pasties must be more than ready!' she exclaimed with a laugh, for ten minutes had stretched into twenty, and she hurriedly left Verity sipping the remains of her sherry. Once eaten, they settled themselves with a cup of tea in the small comfy wooden arm chairs to each side of the new labour-saving gas fire which Octavia would have welcomed on that bitterly cold winter Kitty was born when the coal fire needed constant attention to keep it burning night and day.

Verity stared blindly into her cup until Octavia renewed the conversation that died as they left the table.

'I hope you won't mind me asking Verity, but are you alright? You don't seem yourself at all today?'

Verity dragged her eyes from her tea and looked across steadily into Octavia's questioning ones and nervously cleared her throat.

'No, I'm not. It's….it's… all very difficult.'

'Whatever is it Verity?'

'I hardly know how to tell you this and the only reason it hasn't been said before is because none of us wished for you to be hurt and upset, particularly after the terrible accident to Kitty and all the stress and worry you have had to deal with since then.'

At Verity's pale and tense look and unnerved at her words, Octavia braced herself.

'Whatever it is you're trying to say, I can see it's not easy, but for goodness sake spit it out!'

'Yes, I must,' Verity replied with an unexpected rush of resolution coursing through her and she plunged on. 'You asked me last week if I knew anyone called Madeline and I denied knowing her. Well, I'm afraid I lied.'

Octavia stared uncomprehendingly at her.

'The truth of the matter is I knew Madeline when she was a little girl. I met her and her mother Faith on the boat going home from Malaysia just after war broke out. Eventually they came to live with me in Penzance to escape the bombing of London and after the war they returned to Malaysia as I did a little later with Maurice when he became well enough to travel. What I have to tell you, and it upsets me to do this, is that James had an affair with Faith and Madeline is his daughter.'

There was a sharp intake of breath from Octavia who sat motionless for several minutes. Verity could see a sweep of emotions across her heart shaped face as the implications began to sink in. The tick of the grandfather clock sounded loud in the silence of the room and the atmosphere became charged with hostility.

'I see,' Octavia said finally. 'So now you admit you know Madeline and her mother, intimately it would seem, and yet didn't think fit to tell me, even after I'd asked if you'd heard of her.' Octavia's eyes burned with the accusation but Verity held her gaze and her ground.

'I know and I hated lying. It's not in my nature to but I was asked by Terry to keep his confidence that he was once engaged to Kitty because Madeline, until recently, had no idea she had a half-sister—'

'But what has Terry to do with this girl?'

'He married her,' she replied quietly.

Octavia's head snapped back into the chair. She stared at Verity in disbelief. '*Married* her!'

'Yes, and the reason Kitty has been asking to see Madeline is because she's known about her for some time. She found out from me when I went to stay with them on the mine. I saw a photo of Kitty's father James in her family album and was dumbfounded to see it was Maurice's friend during the war and the man Faith had an affair with. I knew then that Madeline and Kitty were half-sisters. A lot came to light that evening, including Kitty's admission of having seen Faith dancing with James in one of her time-slips....'

Octavia tutted. 'I've never believed in that sort of thing.'

'Well, be that as it may, Kitty knew of my friendship with Faith and of her daughter and having been mistaken for Madeline by her friends and even by me, it didn't take her long to work out that Madeline was her half-sister. Of course, I couldn't deny it. Later, when Kitty came home to have her baby, she confided in Terry and your husband Jack about James's affair. I think she was curious to meet Madeline but out of loyalty to you decided against it, and your husband

174

agreed it should remain in the past as you had already suffered enough.'

'How typical of Jack. Let sleeping dogs lie. Everyone else can know about James's philandering but me.' Octavia's mouth closed in a tight line of resentment.

'I can understand how you must be feeling and I'm so sorry to be the bearer of such upsetting revelations,' said Verity. 'I value our friendship very much and never intended to deceive you in any way, none of us did. This whole matter has come about by keeping things from one another for the most compassionate of reasons.

But Octavia was barely listening with the dawning realization Terry's parents would have also been told about James's infidelity. It was common knowledge. How utterly humiliating. She felt her mind and body shutting down at the thought.

Verity knew there was nothing more she could do or say to alleviate Octavia's distress. She rose to leave. 'Under the circumstances, I think it best my dear to leave you with your thoughts and I'll see Kitty next week. I hope you will forgive me for bringing such painful news.'

Octavia did not resist her suggestion and began to rise shakily to her feet. 'I'll get your coat.'

'No need, just rest in the chair, and I'll make you a fresh pot of tea before I go and although I know you don't take sugar in your tea, maybe a spoonful of it today wouldn't go amiss. You've had an awful blow.'

Tea was the British answer to all ails, catastrophes and wars, Octavia thought mindlessly.

'Will you be all right?' Verity asked, her pale blue eyes filled with kindly concern at leaving her. 'I will stay if you wish?'

'That's good of you, Verity but I'll be fine, and believe me I'm not annoyed with you. I can see these things had to be said and I'm sorry I snapped.'

'You had every right to react in anger. You wouldn't be human if you didn't. Now, I'll go out and make the tea, and then I'll take a turn around Camborne town before I catch the train. You have some very nice shops to browse.'

Octavia sat drinking her tea reflecting on the coincidence of James meeting Verity's husband Maurice during the war, and numb with the discovery that James had another daughter. Her sympathies lay with Verity who had been put into an impossible position. It took courage to admit to her she had lied, even though it was for the best of intentions. As she looked back on her marriage to James, common sense began to override her anger at his adultery. After all, she conceded, she barely knew him. They were married for one short month before he left for Malaysia with only letters to sustain her newly married status. In many ways it was not surprising he had met someone when mining engineers were contracted to work for three years abroad before wives could join them. A misguided system if ever there was one. She suddenly recalled her disquiet on his return from his tour before the war took him away again. He was distracted and distant. So that was what it was about, another women and a daughter in his life and she had been foolish enough to think it was the fear of what the future held with a war looming. Thirty years and more had passed since her marriage to James and she was fortunate to later have the safe haven of Jack until he was so cruelly taken from her.

She stared unseeing at the fire. One thing she had learnt over the years, life was never fair. She would have to accept she must meet Kitty's half-sister if it meant a chance of helping Kitty to recover her memory. It went against the grain, although she could hardly blame the girl for being born, and in any case, what choice did she have with Kitty asking to see her and Terry on a daily basis? It was a blessing that Kitty only remembered him from childhood and not as the man with whom she fell in love. Having made the decision Octavia felt strength and purpose returning to her, and getting up from her chair went into the hallway and telephoned May: her lifeline, always.

'May is there any chance you could come up with Amy today instead of tomorrow? I have just heard something that you probably won't be surprised to hear, and I need to talk it over with you.

Chapter Seventeen

A SOBER LITTLE group made their way along the terrace to Octavia's house, Verity and Madeline walking to each side of Terry who was pushing Robert in his pushchair. Their conversation died away as they neared the gate and Madeline's mouth was dry with anxiety.

Sitting with May in the bay window of the front room waiting for them to arrive, Octavia was equally on tenterhooks. She took comfort that May was with her and May was more than intrigued to meet Kitty's sister. Amy, sitting on the carpet with the little cot that Terry's father had made for Kitty when she was born, was busily crooning to her doll and feeding her with a bottle. They watched her, glad of the light diversion. Amy feeling their eyes upon her held up her dolly for them to see she was now ready for bed.

'I was right, wasn't I May to delay her meeting the rest of the family?' Octavia said suddenly. 'It would have been daunting for her.'

May could feel the worry and tension in the air and reassured her.

'Of course you were. It was the most sensible thing to do. It's best to take this one step at a time. There will be another day when we can get together and she can meet everyone else.' She glanced back out of the window. 'Oh, my Lord! Here they come!' she exclaimed.

Octavia's eyes flew to the terrace, watching them intently on their drawing near to the gate. 'Verity's right. There is a resemblance to Kitty,' she said, with a catch in her throat.

'May, this feels very strange,' and went to open the door.

'Hello, my dear,' said Verity, standing at the head of the little entourage. 'Well, here we are! I thought the front door today!' she whispered whilst Terry fiddled to undo the restraining straps and lifted Robert from the chair.

Octavia smiled in agreement and opened the door wide for the pushchair.

Madeline gave Octavia a hesitant look and swung the chair over the step and into the entrance porch.

Terry greeted her with a quiet 'Hello, Mrs. Pengelly. How are you?'

'Flummoxed!'

Terry flushed. Octavia had lost none of her sharp repartee. He turned to May who was standing with a welcoming smile behind Octavia in the hallway passage.

'Hello Terry. Long time, no see.'

'Yes, well, you know how it is, business keeps me busy.'

May had never seen Terry looking so ill at ease. She had known him since a boy growing up with Kitty with his laid-back way and warm smile, but now he was acting like a stranger and seemingly lost for conversation. Still, it was understandable she supposed given the circumstances. She glanced at Octavia who also appeared momentarily at a loss.

'Please, come in everyone and take a pew,' May invited.

'Yes, come in,' Octavia said, following May's cue and leading them into the front room.

Amy raised her arms to May to be lifted, shy of the sudden influx of people. May picked her up onto her

179

hip with a smile at her and said to no-one in particular, 'This is Amy, Kitty's daughter.'

There was an awkward hiatus of movement until Verity said, 'Madeline, I'd like you to meet Octavia.'

They shook hands warily. 'Hello Madeline. It's nice to meet you, although I wish it were under happier circumstances.'

'Yes, so do I, Mrs. Pengelly,' Madeline responded with a sympathetic half-smile.

'And this must be Robert?' said Octavia, turning to Terry who was holding him. 'What a beautiful little boy.'

'Thank you,' Madeline replied, her face lighting up with pride and love.

Terry set Robert down when he immediately crawled over to Amy and sitting on his padded bottom stared wide-eyed at her. She studied him back and deciding he was a worthy recipient of her possessions, offered him one of her cloth picture books, but Robert had seen her pull-along duck and was onto all fours in a second, pushing it speedily along as he crawled. Amy, seeing it rapidly disappearing before her, caught hold of the trailing string and pulled hard. Robert letting out a wail of protest, held grimly on to the duck. The tense atmosphere in the room relaxed and sitting down there was laughter at this tussle between them. Terry turning to Verity said how Amy looked a lot like Kitty when she was a little girl, and of course, the family likeness was there with the two sisters. There was a general murmur of agreement.

Octavia looking around at this mix of family and friends had the oddest sensation of being in a bubble of unreality to see Madeline, the mirror image of Kitty, with Terry who had been in and out of her home since a boy.

'I'm so sorry to hear of Kitty's accident Mrs. Pengelly and I do so hope by seeing us both it will help in her recovery,' said Madeline.

'Yes, so do I. It was a terrific shock for the family,' Octavia replied, recovering herself, 'but the more we can do to bring her back into the present, the better. I've been warned it may take years or it may never happen. We live from day to day. She has no memory of Amy or Lawrence, I'm afraid, and only remembers her childhood with us and of course you, Terry. It will not be the Kitty you remember, so do be prepared.'

'I understand. I realise it's not going to be an easy meeting.'

'Well, we shall see but I think seeing you will give her a lot of happiness.'

Octavia looked at Madeline with interest thinking how attractive she looked in a flared white cotton-print dress with sprigs of green leaves. Around her waist was a contrasting narrow belt of yellow that emphasised her neat figure and her slim legs finished with white low heeled shoes. She carried a matching yellow handbag and had the same distinct strawberry blond hair that was continuing down through the next generation of James's family.

'It will be interesting to see how she responds to you, Madeline. The knowledge that she had a half-sister has not been lost, despite her catastrophic head injury. It really is quite incredible.'

***

Terry felt a shiver of déjà vu as they entered the reception hall where Kitty had seen the Christmas tree and the ghost children. He wondered whether Kitty still saw them, and hoped with her mind so affected by the accident she no longer did, or heard the desperate cries of the two little girls in a trunk in the store room at the top of the house. He remembered how eerie it had been for Kitty to discover years later from Phoebe that one of them was James's sister Mary who died when playing hide and seek with the owner's daughter Victoria. It was little wonder Octavia hated the house and warned him and Kitty to stay away from it when they were children.

Nurse Thomas appeared from the dining room with its dark linen-fold panelling, now converted into an office and rest room for the staff.

'Hello, Mrs. Pengelly, Mrs. Nicholls. Lovely weather today.'

'Yes it is. So how is our Kitty today?'

'I'm please to say in the last day or two she has improved tremendously. She can now fully dress herself and because of this is less frustrated and aggressive and we have been able to reduce her medication.'

'That's wonderful news nurse,' Octavia replied. She touched Terry's arm and drew him to her side. 'This is Terry who, as you know, Kitty has been asking to see. Living next door to us they were inseparable as children, and this is his wife Madeline, Kitty's half-sister.

'Nurse Thomas's face expressed surprise. 'My goodness! You are so like Kitty. You could almost be twins. Kitty is sitting as always in her favourite place overlooking the garden Mrs. Pengelly. Let me take you all to her.'

Terry gazed around the room he remembered so clearly the day they broke into Nancarrow. Gone was the stamp of a gentleman's room with the heavy mahogany desk and display case, the world globe, the library of books and the high leather-backed chair where Kitty said she could smell pipe smoke. In their place were comfortable arm chairs and low coffee tables, and the walls where the book shelves once rose to the ceiling were now painted in pale gold with touches of restful prints of Cornwall. Hearing their voices Kitty looked around, her face breaking into a smile for Octavia and Verity.

'Hello Kitty,' Octavia said kissing her. 'Look who I've brought to see you. You remember Terry, don't you?'

Terry surprised at Octavia's outward show of affection for Kitty waited before stepping forward, and submitting a kiss to her cheek found he was seized with profound pity for the girl he once loved. She was painfully thin, her cheeks hollowed out and her beautiful green eyes lacked their depth of fire he had lost his heart to, but as he searched her face, he could see a semblance of the old Kitty fighting to emerge from the fog that was crippling her abilities to look after herself and recall her married life.

'Hello Kitty,' he said. 'It's good to see you again.'

She stared at him and Terry saw how hard she was trying to remember, and then her wide generous mouth broke into a smile of sheer delight.

'Terry! Terry!' she exclaimed. 'You're back from Exeter!'

'Yes, that's right. How are you?' he asked, smiling down at her.

Seeing her sister, their physical likeness to one another took Madeline's breath away, and it pricked her with a small flutter of fear as she watched Terry taking Kitty's hand.

'I'm much better, thank you, aren't I, mum?' she enthused, looking up at Octavia.

'Yes, you certainly are,' Octavia agreed with a positive note in her voice. 'And I hear from nurse you're now dressing yourself without any help.'

'Yes! It's easy-peasy!'

Terry's heart jolted at the childhood memory; words they said to encourage one another when facing a challenge.

'Now Kitty, there's someone I want you to meet.' He sought Madeline's hand and pulled her to his side. 'You once said to me that you would like to meet your half-sister Madeline, well here she is!'

Kitty's response was so startling, it astounded them all. For one radiant moment it seemed Kitty was whole again. She moved without effort to her feet and flung her arms around Madeline, holding her to her own thin form, her face animated with joy, her words slurring with excitement when they stepped apart.

'I'm so happy to see you.' She turned to Verity and said, 'M-a-d-e-l-i-n-e saved me from d-r-o-w-n-i-n-g in the sea!'

Holding her hands tightly, Madeline smiled back. 'And I'm so happy to see you too, Kitty,' and saw in her eyes a spark of recognition, and then it was gone. Had Kitty for that split second remembered her from that day on the platform at St. Ives and felt too the bond between them?

Nurse Thomas reappeared with the tea trolley and they were grateful for the timely interruption of a difficult moment and Kitty overwhelmed with happiness felt for her chair and sat down abruptly.

Madeline cast a quizzical look at Terry and whispered, 'Saved her from the sea!?'

'I'll explain later.'

'You know what's happened, don't you?' Terry said to Octavia and Verity under his breath, in the activity of drawing up chairs around Kitty. 'She's confusing the

184

two, her lost twin and her half-sister. They've become one in her mind.'

'How on earth do I deal with this mix-up?' Octavia murmured to Verity. 'Her mind is all over the place.'

'By acceptance for the time being. There's nothing else you can do other than to keep speaking of Madeline as her sister,' Verity replied, looking fondly across at Kitty. 'It's wonderful to see her so happy after weeks of mood swings and struggling to recover from her terrible injuries. I can hardly believe the difference today.'

'Neither can I,' replied Octavia watching Terry and Madeline with their heads close to Kitty who was listening to him recalling childhood escapades that had her giggling and her words tripping over themselves in her eagerness to join in. She was bright with a happiness they'd not seen since her return home.

'I only wish May was here to see this,' Octavia said, 'but she felt it would have been too many people for Kitty at one time and she was tickled pink at the idea of looking after a baby again. She loves the babyhood.'

'Verity chuckled 'She'll have her hands full if the tussle between them was anything to go by!'

Octavia laughingly agreed with her eyes on Kitty. 'It's good to see the young couple with her, Verity. You were right to bring everything out into the open. I do hope this meeting will help Kitty gain ground. She may never recover her memory of Lawrence or Amy, but once she's home, she'll be surrounded by the love of the family who will all help to look after her. I've a suspicion Kitty will come to think of Amy as her baby sister!' With a wry look she said,

'It would have to have been an immaculate conception!' and they tittered together.

The visiting time passed quickly and before long Terry and Madeline rose from their chairs.

185

'We should be leaving Mrs. Pengelly. We must give Robert his tea before we catch the train, and relieve May from looking after him. It was so good of her to offer to do that.'

'No. Don't go, don't go,' Kitty pleaded with them, crying and holding onto their hands.

Seeing her agitation Octavia said, 'I'll stay behind for a little while. You go ahead with Verity. I know May will have tea waiting. I'll join you later.'

'Kitty we have to go now,' Terry said, kissing her goodbye, 'but we will see you again soon, I promise. I'm working now so it's not always easy to get away, but we shall come back as often as we can.'

'Yes, we will,' Madeline agreed. 'You see, today we have a train to catch to Penzance where we live, but when we come next time, we shall bring our little boy Robert to show you. Would you like that?'

Kitty nodded a whispered, 'Yes,' and looked so forlorn on their waving to her from the door, that once outside, Madeline's eyes filled with tears.

'Oh Terry. The poor little soul. Her bones may have healed but what is her mind still going through?'

'I dread to think,' Terry replied. 'To see Kitty like that is the saddest sight I have ever seen,' and holding Madeline's hand tightly, they walked out of Nancarrow and up the hill.

***

It seemed to Octavia after Terry and Madeline's first visit to Nancarrow and subsequent ones, they were the spur to Kitty's progress. By the beginning of November she was walking without a frame, her speech therapist had alleviated the slurring of her words and she was able, in her limited way, to take care of herself. She was reading books by authors she had once loved; Enid Blyton whose *Secret Seven* story was her inspiration for forming with her childhood friends her Secret Service Society, and Susan Coolridge's *What Katy Did* books when, as a child, she had identified and considered herself more than equal to Katy's tomboy adventures. With her improvement, the doctor suggested a trial run at home.

Kitty was jubilant to be back in familiar surroundings. In her old bedroom she delved into her childhood jewellery box, discovering trinkets and treasures kept as keepsakes, and she was overjoyed at finding the angel's feather from Porthcurnow.

But as the week went by Octavia found she could be volatile and unpredictable, and when she misplaced a little gold cross that May had given her for her twelfth birthday, was quick to anger.

'You left it in on your dressing table Kitty. You haven't lost it.'

Kitty hastened up the stairs and on retrieving it, sat moodily in the front room chair and stared out over the field to Nancarrow. 'I don't want to go back there,' she said pointing to the outline of the house through the bare branches of the trees.

Octavia left her and fetched the radio from the kitchen, fearing to antagonize her into a further outburst of opposition if she mentioned returning there for a final assessment. She switched it on hoping the music would stir her memory to happier times when she would sing and dance along to the popular tunes of the day. Kitty ignored it, putting her hands over her ears and growling to herself. Octavia felt a pang of despair. She was warned by the doctor of personality changes that came with a head trauma and he was right. To all intents and purposes she appeared perfectly normal apart from those closest to her who soon found she was not the spirited Kitty they remembered; her attention span was short and her mind and conversation was that of a ten year old. She was glad she had suggested for May, Ted and Helen to come up today for tea. She needed their normality and support and the pleasure of watching her granddaughter playing with her toys and beginning to say her words.

***

Kitty licked the spoon after stirring the Christmas cake mixture. The smells of the spices and fruits flooded her head with memories. 'When can we decorate the tree with daddy?'

Octavia's heart stopped. She had managed to pacify Kitty's questions about Jack by saying he was away working on Mining School business in London to explain his absence from seeing her, and had anxiously wondered how long it would take for Kitty to become aware he still wasn't around. She could not beat about the bush any longer.

'Daddy died three years ago, Kitty.'

'That's not true! You said he was away working.'

How could her memory be so fiendishly accurate to remember that, and yet unable to remember even the simplest things like where she had left her necklace? Octavia thought despairingly.

'Yes, I know I did, but you have been very sick and I wanted you to get better first before telling you.'

'He didn't die!' Her voice rose and Octavia's stomach sank with the fear of another hysterical outburst. 'You're making it up.'

'No I'm not,' Octavia replied, keeping her voice calm. 'He had a stroke. It was very sudden.'

'You're lying! It's not true. It's not true,' she screamed. 'I hate you.' She flung the spoon onto the floor and slammed out of the kitchen and up the stairs with a thumping of angry feet to her bedroom. How right May's impulsive offer had been to look after Amy, she thought, and how she desperately needed to talk over her concerns with the doctor. She went to the bottom of the stairs.

'Kitty, come down here. I need to give you your medicine,' she called up.

'No, I don't want to,' Kitty yelled back.

Exasperated, Octavia went up the stairs and stood in the doorway of her room where Kitty had flung herself onto the bed.

'Now you know the doctor said you must take it every day and if you don't, you will have to go back to Nancarrow and you don't want that, do you?'

A reluctant Kitty followed Octavia back down the stairs and into the kitchen, and sullen faced, swallowed her pills.

Octavia decided that for once she would not pacify and would try a firm stand, as she would do to any ten year old. 'I know it's a terrible shock hearing about daddy, but I will not be screamed or shouted at again. Do you understand?'

'Yes,' she said glaring at her and then her face crumpled. 'I want daddy.'

'I know you do, and I'm so sorry Kitty that daddy isn't here any more. I want him too. I miss him very much and so do Thomas and Grace. Look, why don't you go up into the sitting room by the fire and I'll find some doilies for you to colour-in like you used to do for our Sunday tea.' She hunted through the cabinet drawer and pulled out a pack of them.

'Here we are, take them with you and pick out the pattern you like best. Your coloured pencils are on the table. I'll bring up a glass of Dandelion and Burdock and tea for me, and we can have a nice afternoon together in front of the fire with you colouring your doily and me reading my new Woman's Own magazine.'

Kitty turned compliantly from the kitchen. The set of her body and face was one of such dejection Octavia could have cried for her. It was one more hurdle Kitty would have to overcome.

The next day Kitty was quiet and Octavia tried to lift her spirits by talking about the forthcoming carol and nativity service in Camborne church, at which she brightened, and said how much she was waiting to see everyone on Christmas day, especially Robert to whom she had taken a particular shine.

'Robert is your nephew Kitty. That's because Madeline is your sister,' she said, reinforcing the relationship like Verity suggested. She had thought of saying half-sister, but it was early days for complicated family clarifications. She was confused enough as it was, although now she was home Kitty had thankfully not made any further reference to Madeline being her guardian angel.

With the whole family together for Christmas Day, it was a day of happiness and laughter, the only sadness being that Jack was not there to share it with them. In place of Jack, Thomas had helped Kitty to decorate the tree that stood in the bay where it was always placed at Christmas time. Kitty insisted on the big red and yellow paper bell hanging in the centre of the ceiling with the Chinese lanterns swinging in loops across the room, although Octavia would have preferred keeping the decorations simple like she had done in past years, but it was important for them all to keep Kitty on an even keel with everything as she remembered it.

May, Ted and Helen arrived with Amy and armfuls of her gifts from Santa and joined the rest of the family sitting around the fire with a glass of port. Amy came to each in turn, proudly showing them her new toys. Grace told her she look prettier than the fairy on the tree all dressed up in her red velvet smocked dress that Octavia had made. With a shy smile she showed it off, twirling around and around, aware of being the centre of attention and the cause of their laughter.

'We have some presents for you too, Amy.' Octavia took her hand. 'Now what do we have here hiding away under the tree? Look! Lots of presents all for Amy!'

Unsure, Amy looked at May and Ted who encouraged her to tear off the wrapping papers with granny. The Oooohs and Ahhhhs of merriment came from the family with each unveiling, the first being Uncle Thomas's gift of a ball with cut out shapes to push through the apertures, a humming top from Aunty Grace and Uncle Chris. Amy self-consciously hid her face in her hands amongst her toys, and Octavia swept her into her arms with a wave of tenderness for her granddaughter so fair and sweet, and covered the baby silkiness of her cheeks with raspberry kisses until Amy giggled and squirmed to be released to the laughter of the family.

Octavia watched Kitty hand Amy her gift of a toy telephone and hid her sadness that Kitty thought of her as a sister, and went around to the back of the tree where she had hidden her gift of a soft horse push-along walker from herself.

At tea time, as arranged, Terry's parents came from next door with Terry, Madeline and baby Robert to join them for Christmas Day and bringing Verity who they had invited to stay over with the family. They arrived wreathed in smiles and grateful the awkwardness of the past that had blighted their neighbourly friendship was now put behind them. They insisted she must not hesitate to ask for help if needed, for they realized the difficulties that Octavia must be experiencing and she thanked them for their understanding and kindness and for always being such good neighbours.

'What would I have done without you all those years ago in that bitter winter when Kitty was born?' Octavia said.

It was a long hard winter that year, they agreed, and as one, gazed at Kitty playing with Amy, surrounded by those that loved her and remembering how she used to be; the tomboy who played with their son, who loved and then left him, and who was now a child again. The path of life was unfathomable for who could have predicted their son would find happiness with Kitty's half-sister, or how the ties of family and friendship now bound them inextricably together.

Chapter Eighteen

Easter 1973

'I WAS ENGAGED to Terry! Why didn't I marry him?' Kitty suddenly announced to the table where Grace, Chris and Thomas had joined them for Easter Sunday lunch. They were eating their traditional roast of Cornish lamb and home grown mint that Kitty had made into a sauce; a chore she had loved to do before her marriage, taking pleasure in the aromatic scent of the mint being chopped.

The gentle buzz of family conversation died and knives and forks dropped onto plates. They all gazed at Kitty with a mix of surprised delight and apprehension, and then to Octavia for her reaction. So, she thought, it has finally happened, as the neurosurgeon had advised, the step by slow step return of her memory. Octavia felt hope swing through her body.

'Kitty, you didn't marry Terry because you met someone else and married him. He was called Lawrence. Do you remember him?' she said cautiously.

Kitty thought hard.

'No, I don't.'

Octavia feeling it was an opportune moment to try and stir her memory with other details of her life with Lawrence, asked her, 'Perhaps you can remember going to live in Malaysia and that you had a daughter called Amy who's now sitting beside you?'

Amy looked up at mother with an earnest expression. 'It's true, you are my mummy,' for Octavia had never made a secret of the fact to Amy that Kitty was her mother.

Kitty frowned. 'You're both being silly. Amy's my sister!' she huffed.

'Well, I can understand why you would think that Kitty but the truth is you were married to Lawrence and you were both in a car accident in Malaysia. I'm afraid Lawrence died. Verity flew home with you and Amy and as you know, you were very poorly and had to be nursed in Nancarrow.'

'So I lived in Malaysia? Is this true?' she asked doubtfully to Thomas and Grace across the table.

'Yes Kitty,' replied Thomas. 'What mum said did happen, only you can't remember it which is quite common after an accident. I expect the memory of Lawrence and your life there will return eventually, like you've just remembered you were engaged to Terry.'

'Yes, it's sure to happen with you being so much better,' joined in Grace quickly, seeing the signs that Kitty was becoming agitated, 'and we're all so pleased that you're home again with us. Mum said you made Russian Crème today for afters. You always were a dab hand at that.'

Taking their cue from Grace, the conversation was steered into safer waters on seeing Kitty retreating into herself.

As the family chatter resumed, Octavia was thinking of another Easter after Kitty was born, when new life was burgeoning from the earth, as it was now, in beacons of light from daffodils and with the first hint of bluebells in the woods. She remembered Nurse Richards who came daily during those long snow-bound days and nights to attend to Kitty and looking down into her cot where for months she had made no sound or movement, said, "It's time you stirred your stumps, my lady" and within days she responded, mewing like a kitten and kicking with her matchstick legs. At six months it was Kitty's first display of a spark of life and was ready join the world outside after her birth when she weighed little more than a bag of sugar. It seemed on this Easter Sunday Octavia once again had been given another small sign. Kitty was coming back to them.

The letter came out of the blue.

11 Asley Grove,
Birmingham.
10th June 1973

Dear Aunt Octavia,

It has been a long time I know since you've heard from me and can only plead that I was never a good letter writer which of course is no excuse. However, dad keeps me up to date with your news and I hear that Kitty is so much better these days and has recovered more of her memory. That is wonderful news.

I don't know if dad has told you or not, but now that I've finished my training as a doctor and intern, I've been thinking of working as a G.P. in a practice in Cornwall. I have never forgotten our holidays there or our stay with you when Diane was so ill, and dad brought John and me down to give mum a break. It was a time that stands out clear in my memory, not to mention your wonderful pasties!

Anyway the reason I'm writing is to ask if there is any chance I could stay with you for a few days – from 1st July until 5th when I have interviews to attend and it would be lovely to see you and the family again. The surgery is in Penzance, a very busy one from all accounts and I can think of no better a place to live if I obtain the post.

I trust this finds you well and, I would imagine, kept very busy with little Amy to look after as well as her mother. Dad has talked of visiting Cornwall with mum many times, but once John and I flew the coop, they never seemed to get around to it. If I'm fortunate enough to come down and live there, they will have no reason not to visit!

Dad sends his love and best wishes as do I,

Peter

Octavia sat with the letter in her hand at the kitchen table. Her thoughts went back to the year of nineteen fifty one when she received his father's letter and how she had baulked at her cousin Roy's request to come and stay, thinking of the extra work and cooking. Thomas was still a baby and she'd worried about how she could sleep eight in three bedrooms. Jack, sitting opposite her across the breakfast table was persuasive; it would do her good to see her cousin Roy and his sons John and Peter after the hardship of the war years, and with Roy's company car, he could take her and the children on outings and think what a wonderful change that would be from catching buses and trains. He was so sickeningly positive she'd given in for everyone's sake, not least for the girls who with the exciting thought of a car right outside their front door, had been listening with bated breath for her decision.

The week had proved memorable and not simply for the pleasure of trips out to beaches and coves that were off the beaten track. Peter had broken his arm during their week with them, and John arrived withdrawn and uncommunicative until Kitty with her unerring instinct realized something was making him desperately unhappy. Jack had seen her sitting with him on the rocks at Porthcurnow beach, their heads close together talking, but it was not until they had returned home to Birmingham that Kitty repeated to Jack, with no understanding of what she was revealing, the conversation she had had with John. It was then they understood with alarm the reason for John's low spirits; the shocking discovery of his sport's teachers sordid behaviour to him. John was such a nice quietly mannered boy, and it upset her to think about it, even now. The situation had been resolved by their writing to Roy, who on the school board of governors, had acted quickly and discovered this was not the first time the headmaster had been approached with a similar complaint by a boy's parents, and the teacher was dismissed. What would have happened if it had not been for Kitty's dogged persistence in wheedling it out of him and the timely intervention before any lasting damage had been done, she dreaded to think. He certainly seemed a lot happier the following year racing around on the beach when Roy and the whole family came down and stayed for a week in a hut on Gwithian towans.

On this occasion the transferring of sleeping arrangements would be easy. Amy could move in with Kitty in Grace's old bed, and Peter could sleep in her small front bedroom, and with a doctor in the house what could possibly go wrong, although she ought to know by now never to tempt fate. It had a way of biting back at her. Still, it would be interesting to see how Peter as a newly qualified doctor found Kitty. When they were children, their relationship appeared to be a love-hate one. Peter was competitive and Kitty wanting to prove she was as good as any boy set out to win whether playing board games or in physical activity. A close eye had to be kept on both of them for Kitty matched Peter's adventurous spirit to the point of danger when the two families linked up for days together on Roy's annual holiday. In their late teenage years, Peter and John looked to new vistas and climes with their friends to the immense disappointment of Kitty who loved the reckless courage Peter brought with him, and soon after, even his occasional scrappy letters of his life in Birmingham, dried up. Peter was, as he confessed, a poor letter writer.

Kitty came into the kitchen. 'Who's the letter from?' she asked, seeing it lying on the table.

'It's from your cousin Peter asking if he could come and stay for a few days in July. Do you remember him?'

'How could I forget Peter! He was a right little tearaway. He broke his arm when they came to stay here. The rope swing snapped in two when we were both swinging on it in Nancarrow woods and he wasn't able to go on the rough rides at Whitsun Fair the next day because his arm was in plaster.' She grinned at the memory. 'He was spitting mad at that and so jealous when I rode with John on the ghost train ride.'

Octavia thought how attractive she looked in her blue and mauve print hot pants outfit with a matching wrap around skirt. She wore knee high white boots ready for the walk down the hill to spend a day with May before picking Amy up from school, taking her there for tea and then coming home together. She had regained her weight, and one wet afternoon curled up on the settee reading, said she had decided to change her long hair to a short cut with flicks around her face, it was all the rage, showing Octavia pictures in the Woman's Own magazine. It suited her for the cut emphasised her high cheek bones and eyes which had finally lost their haunted look. Octavia found each passing year she was taking small steps to normality, although she could not ignore the changes to Kitty's personality. There were still the occasional outbursts of temper and lack of concentration and she was slower in her speech, but as she studied her now, the transformation was evident from the desperately sick woman who returned five years ago, reduced to the needs of a baby and having to learn how to walk, talk, bathe and feed herself.

As Octavia foresaw, Kitty looked upon Amy as her little sister, and Amy in her quiet little way with the six sense her mother once possessed, knew something was out of balance with Kitty and remained calm when she lost control of her emotions, and looked after her like a mother hen, fetching and carrying and asking for stories to be read to her, which had the effect of soothing and settling the frustrations that built up in Kitty.

At seven years Amy was a replica of her as a child, light boned and small of build, the copper highlights glinting in her fair hair. It was in her temperament that she differed. Kitty had been daring and reckless, her eyes shining with the chance of adventure which led her to the secrets of Nancarrow and the fear that came with them, but Amy's blue eyes were observant and for a child so young, took a more careful view of the world. May said she was an old soul.

***

Peter drove into the terrace and parking in front of Greenview alighted from the car. The Victorian granite-built house was aptly named he thought, watching the sun chase shadows across the humpy green fields running to the blue of the sea in the far distance. Funny

199

how he hadn't noticed the name before carved into the granite gate post. It was peaceful after the hurly burly of the city, the only sound the soughing of the trees of Nancarrow and the cawing of rooks. It was so familiar it caught at his throat and he had the oddest feeling of having come home. A young face peered out at him from the top bay window giving him a start. It was Kitty! And then she disappeared and he felt foolish mistaking Amy for her mother. He took his jacket and suitcase from the back seat and the front door opened.

Octavia was, as he always remembered her, greeting them from the doorstep on their yearly holidays in Cornwall; a woman made strong from adversity that generated a sense of permanence around her. There were strands of grey here and there now in her short jet black hair, a style she had never changed, and her blue eyes that brooked no nonsense were direct as ever.

'Hello Peter,' she said, as he came up the path and steps to the door. 'Did you have a good journey?'

He hesitated before giving her a peck on the cheek, remembering she was not one for an outward show of affection.

'Yes, on the whole it was a pretty good run down with only one or two hold-ups from road works.'

'It's no small drive from Birmingham,' she acknowledged.

Amy suddenly appeared at her side and gazed up at him.

'This is Amy, Peter. She's been sitting upstairs in my bedroom watching for you, just as Kitty and Grace did when you came down with your father all those years ago.'

'Yes, I saw you, didn't I Amy?'

Amy held out her hand. 'Hello,' he said, taking it. 'I'm your cousin Peter.'

'Shall I call you Uncle Peter?' she asked solemnly, her small hand happy to hold his. Her round blue eyes studied him with curiosity.

'Oh, I think that would do very nicely.'

'I think Kitty would like it too,' she said seriously.

'You mean your mother?'

'Yes, but you see, since the car accident, she thinks I'm her sister. It's all very complicated,' she admitted with a dramatic sigh and a faint rolling of her eyes.

What a quaint little soul, he thought, so utterly different from Kitty, apart from her amazing similarity in looks; the same strawberry blond hair and build, and the most beautiful eyes that viewed the world with a placid acceptance.

Octavia's expression was one of amusement at her granddaughter.

'Kitty's isn't here at the moment. She's gone into town for a freshly baked saffron cake. She remembers how you used to love them. And now you're arrived, I'll put the pasties in the oven, and once they start to brown and smell savoury, you'll know you're in Cornwall!'

Peter gave her a broad smile. 'Nobody makes them like you do, Aunty,' slipping back into his old way of address. He had always found Aunt Octavia a mouthful.

'I'll make us a cup of tea. I expect you could do with one, and if you'd like to take your suitcase upstairs to the small front bedroom whilst I'm doing that, you can settle in.

It had been many years since he'd been to the house, but it was with a sense of familiarity he went up the stairs, poking his head into rooms that seemed smaller than when he was a boy. The house even smelt the same. Odd how all homes did engender a smell of their own. He appreciated what a marvel Octavia had been fitting them all into three bedrooms on their first visit to Cornwall and coping with the extra work and hullaballoo of a houseful of children. He sat down on Amy's pink flamingo bed coverlet engulfed with memories; the first time he had met Kitty at the dining table when she embarrassed Octavia by mentioning the use of their best china and her mother's freezing stare. It could have felled a man. Kitty, he quickly came to appreciate was as reckless as him, testing Jack and Octavia to their exasperated limits; swinging upside down from the lamppost on the terrace, climbing dangerously high rocks, and on the beach she ran like the wind and, to his annoyance, could outdistance him. He smiled at the memory of her absolute belief in mermaids despite his scoffing, and, as if it were yesterday, he remembered the fateful Sunday when they had sneaked off to Nancarrow woods and swung together on a rope swing which parted from the branch of the oak plummeting them to the ground. He had broken his arm and Kitty was convinced it was God's punishment for playing there on a Sunday which was forbidden. In this house Sundays were for church and quiet pursuits. He stood up and looked at Amy's collection of small china animals standing around a mirror on a white painted chest of drawers. He peered closely at a small black and white faded holiday snapshot pushed into the corner of a picture frame of ballerinas hanging on the wall. He wondered if Amy went to ballet classes as Kitty had done. The photograph was taken with Kitty standing on the wild and dramatic Land's End cliffs holding Grace's hand and pleased as punch to be wearing her new shop-bought blue and white polka dot dress that mummy hadn't made, she told him. It was clearly a red letter day. He had a sudden mental image of Octavia sitting on the springing turf with Thomas, not much more than a baby in her lap, and his father Roy standing with them, saying to listen and see if they could hear the ghostly church bells from the land that was said to have disappeared beneath the waves. He moved to the window and looked out to St. Michael's Mount, its outline crystal clear which usually indicated rain was on the way which he hoped for once was wrong. He opened his suitcase and taking out his interview suit and shirt hung them in the single wardrobe. They looked incongruous alongside Amy's dainty dresses, and putting away the rest of his clothes went lightly down the stairs to sit with Amy and Octavia in the front room where a pot of tea awaited.

Amy lay on the floor in the window seemingly engrossed in her colouring-in book, although Peter felt sure her little ears would be well attuned to any conversation.

'This is a lovely room. I hadn't realized it before,' Peter said, sitting down and fully appreciating it for the first time.

'Well, you were only a boy Peter when you came on your holidays to Cornwall. So much has happened in this room,' she reflected. 'For a start, Kitty was born here. I've never wished to live anywhere else, why would I with a view like that,' she indicated with a nod of her head to the window. Once having poured them their tea, she settled into her chair appraising him over her cup. He was dressed casually wearing fashionable slim cut grey trousers with a fine cashmere pullover of green and grey check over a light green shirt. His sharp features were now angled planes, his dark hair cut with a nod to fashion brushed the back of his collar, and his hazel eyes had the brightness of intellect, and she saw too there was kindness.

'Now Peter, I want to hear how the family are going on and all about your training as a doctor. It's a long road and the last occupation I would have expected from you; the services perhaps or maybe the police, anything that involved action!'

Peter laughed. 'I take your point. But before I fill you in on my news and Kitty arrives back from town, tell me, how is she really? Your letter sounded very hopeful.'

'She's doing well and she remembers up to and including her engagement to Terry, but nothing beyond that. Her life in Malaysia seems to have been completely wiped from her mind.'

'That could still return, but from what you have written to me on her progress, the most important aspect of her condition is she's now thinking and functioning as an adult which is good.'

'You're already sounding like a doctor! You haven't been boning up on head injuries by any chance?' she asked with laughter in her eyes.

Peter smiled sheepishly. 'It had occurred to me and I did wonder how she took to finding she had a half-sister who was married to Terry. It must have been quite a shock.'

'Kitty was too ill to understand at the time and the shock was all mine!' she replied with a sharpness that took him back to his childhood visits. 'It shook the whole family, and I would suspect his parents too, although it has never been mentioned between us.'

'Yes, I can imagine it must have been pretty devastating,' he murmured sympathetically with a feeling he had in some subtle way been reprimanded.

'When Kitty met them both she was in the nursing home and very confused and could only recall her childhood. She had driven us mad asking to see Terry and the name Madeline kept cropping up. A name I'd never heard of and it was because of this I learnt from Verity about James and his daughter. So whether I liked it or not, I arranged for Terry and Madeline to see Kitty, anything that might help her to return to the present.'

'It sounds like you've had an awful lot to contend with apart from the consequences of Kitty's car accident.'

'Yes, it hasn't been easy and looking after Kitty was a lot harder than I expected. She was so unpredictable. I couldn't have done it without the help and support of May—'

'I lived with Aunty May for a while,' Amy's young voice butted in from the window.

'Yes, you did, Amy. May rightly pointed out it would impossible for me to cope with a volatile, sick and damaged Kitty and a toddler. Initially I fought the idea, but came to realize she was right. Once Kitty was able to fend for herself, Amy came to me. We are still often caught unawares by Kitty, the last being this Easter when she announced over dinner she had been engaged to Terry and asked us why she hadn't married him. It was the first indication that she was moving from childhood to the present. I explained about Lawrence and the accident but she said she still had no memory of him and refused to accept that Amy was her daughter.

'Even though I told her it was true,' Amy's voice piped up again from the window. 'Lawrence was my daddy, but I don't remember him. Granny says I was too young.'

As Peter surmised, Amy missed little.

'Amy, you must stop interrupting when I'm talking. Just concentrate on colouring in your book.'

It was vintage Octavia, brooking no interference, thought Peter.

'After explaining about Lawrence she did become quiet and you could see she was trying to remember.

205

Incidentally, did she ever say anything to you when you were children about a guardian angel?'

'Not that I can remember.'

'What do you make of such things?'

'I'm not sure really. I'm fairly open-minded about it as I've seen a lot of inexplicable reactions from dying patients. I do recall her saying in Nancarrow garden she saw a little girl who looked like her playing with children all wearing old fashioned clothes by the boathouse. As no-one lived there, it did seem rather odd to me, but I didn't take much notice at the time to be honest. I suppose now I think about it, Kitty did have this fey side to her.' He chuckled. 'But she was also such a tomboy. I'd never met anyone like her. She was a one-off!'

'I can't argue with that!' Octavia said with an old fashioned look.

'The family are all well and send their love. Diane works as a secretary in a solicitor's office and is busy courting, a nice chap that we all like, and John is an accomplished chef. Mum's always ready to hand over the reins in her kitchen when he visits home and we are more than ready to sample his latest concoction. We dine like kings! He said he would like to work in one of the prestigious London hotels for further experience. As for me, my work and training in the hospital is very down to earth and has certainly brought home one's mortality and how life can change at a stroke, both metaphorically and physically.' He grinned. 'Matron is a dragon and breathes fire on the wards, and even the fully qualified surgeons and specialists are terrified of her!'

He stopped at the sound of the back door being opened and footsteps up the passage.

Kitty came into the room with an attractive bloom to her cheeks and breathless from walking the hill. He felt

206

a shock of surprise for quite ridiculously he still thought of her as a teenager and was expecting a shadow of her former self, not this beautiful young woman, He rose rapidly to his feet.

'Peter! My goodness you've grown!' she teased with laughter.

'Now where have I heard that line before?' he grinned back.

'Each year you came down!' she said. They hugged one another laughing. Her body against him was slim and light and, to his intense confusion, utterly desirable. Her eyes were mischievous as they drew apart.

She had completely wrong footed him. 'You're looking well, same old bandy legs I see!' he joked to cover his self-consciousness. 'No scabs on your knees?' peering down at the top of her boots.'

'I should have known better than to have worn hot-pants with you on the scene. You haven't changed a bit. Bandy legs indeed!'

They sat down together laughing, the lost years between them falling away as if they'd never existed, and although he could see there were changes in Kitty, his heart had leapt at the sight of her, and he knew with an absolute certainty he had loved her from their first days together as children. He did not wonder any more as to why he could never commit to women he had known. Not one of them held a candle to Kitty.

And watching them together Octavia felt in her bones they would all be seeing a lot more of Peter.

Chapter Nineteen

ON THIS, HER wedding day, it seemed impossible to believe how ill Kitty had been. Her recovery was a miracle. She looked a picture of serenity as she came down the aisle on Thomas's arm in a floating cream pleated chiffon dress with pearl seeded lace detailing the high neck and cuffs, and waiting for her, Peter thought she had never looked more beautiful. A stir rippled through the church to see Madeline as her Matron of Honour with Grace. Those guests who had not met her could not fail to notice the startling likeness of the half-sisters. There was no getting away from it, she was with all certainty James's daughter. Sympathy had lain for the losses dealt to Octavia over the years, and surprise that she seemed willing to have James's daughter included in the wedding service in such a conspicuous way. But then, it was generally agreed, this was, in the particular, a family whose lives took the most fascinating twists and turns and with this latest unravelling of the past, the town's tongues were busy.

Octavia had no doubt memories would be percolating through their minds seeing the four sisters together once more, her father William's 'harem' who had tripped in and out of the School of Mines – a hotbed of testosterone fuelled young men - where he worked as Registrar. Life had been free and easy then before the onset of war with mining students drawn from across the world, and Alice would marry one and return with him to Greece where he was born. And who could forget the crazy antics of rag week when James took his life in his hands by climbing the School's flag pole to attach to the top a voluminous pair of pink bloomers. She smiled to herself remembering how it generated the town's laughter for weeks flapping in the wind until they became in tatters and were blown away. Such a lot of water had flown under the bridge since then, she reflected, turning to give a smile at Madeline whose head was held high as they drew close to the altar.

Amy, oblivious to everything but her thrill as a bridesmaid was beaming from ear to ear as she walked behind Kitty with her posy of flowers and wearing a dress of silk organza made by Octavia in Amy's favourite colour of pink. It entailed a gracious concession on Madeline's part, who confessed to Terry she felt like an overblown rose dressed in pink; a colour that had never suited her. Taking their vows Octavia offered up her thanks to the Almighty that Kitty would be in safe hands after her initial worry and concerns for her being able to run a home, as well as looking after Amy. She had no qualms for Amy who clearly adored Peter, for after his success of obtaining the general practitioner's post in Penzance, he visited every evening when not on call, and was patient with Kitty in encouraging her to understand and accept she was Amy's mother. At week-ends he took them both out in his car, aware that Amy needed fun time. The unusual circumstances of her childhood had created a serious little girl, responsible beyond her years, who had had to accept a back seat with care concentrated on helping Kitty to recover, although Peter acknowledged Amy could not have been loved or safeguarded more than by her Granny and Aunty May. Octavia thought it only fair to warn Peter that Kitty could still flair up in a temper over nothing and from time to time suffered from severe migraine type headaches. He told her not to worry, he fully understood the difficulties, after all he was a doctor now, he said with an indulgent grin at her, and nodding her head in agreement, Octavia said she knew she was being silly and worrying for nothing.

'No, not for nothing, Aunty. You've been through a great deal of anguish and strain pulling Kitty through the complications of recovery so you're bound to have concerns about Kitty being able to cope on her own. And she will, I promise you. I will never let any harm come to her or Amy.'

Nevertheless she was going to find it hard to let them go.

Octavia was not quite sure how she managed to net her sister Phoebe for Kitty's wedding with her flitting from country to country under the guise of an attaché for the Foreign Office. Tall with a boyish figure that lent itself to uniform and well-cut clothes, and with her trade mark of simple yet stylish hats, beneath which her feline eyes gave nothing away, she was a striking presence. Today she was wearing a black and white silk dress, a simple and classic cut that hugged her figure and fell in soft folds from the waist and with her matching picture hat partly hiding her face and eyes was a perfect reflection of her persona, Octavia thought.

Phoebe was also thinking of the strange twists and turns life took as her eyes travelled around family and friends jostling together for the photographer. Who would have thought that one woman by her wonderful care and friendship of two sisters had led to this gathering; that Peter would return to Cornwall and marry Kitty and that they would be living in Penzance as Madeline did with Terry. Perhaps Kitty was right there were no such things as coincidences but a divine plan revealed to us through choices and circumstances.

She had been as horrified as Octavia on seeing Kitty on her return from Malaysia and could scarcely believe her to be the same young woman who first confided in her and sought her advice on her dilemma of having to tell Terry that she wished to break off her engagement to him after falling in love with Lawrence. It was now six years since that fateful car accident, and against all the odds, Kitty had healed which in no small way she accepted was due to the love and nursing care Octavia had given her.

She watched her sister Octavia talking playfully to Amy and could see the years of looking after Kitty had taken their toll, and guilt sliced through her for not making more of an effort to have come down. Hers was a shadowy world where she had learnt to keep her composure and emotions in check and more particularly after James's betrayal of her love whilst she was away at university, and discovered James had turned his considerable charm and good looks onto a young and unworldly Octavia. Phoebe fled Cornwall and made her life in London, breaking off contact until time lessoned the pain and there had been forgiveness. In the end Phoebe thought with irony, they had both lost him, and for Octavia with this late knowledge of James's affair, it came twice over. It surprised her not in the least to hear from May that James had had a daughter in Malaysia. The discovery must have been devastating for Octavia and without Jack's loving support - dear Jack who was taken far too soon - it would have been a bitter pill to swallow. Phoebe speculated on how Octavia would cope with Kitty and Amy leaving home. Peter had assured her Amy was earmarked to be spending a lot of time with her granny and for that, Phoebe was placated, for under Octavia's hard shell exterior her little granddaughter was the soft chocolate centre of her life.

Kitty gazed out across the reception room buzzing with happy chatter and laughter as her guests enjoyed their wedding breakfast. Her eyes rested on Terry sitting with his parents who clearly doted on their grandson Robert sitting beside them. Memories of their childhood escapades brought a smile to her lips. His love for her had never wavered since the day they broke into Nancarrow, when their friendship changed into an unshakeable love as children and deepened with the years into an engagement. How could she have betrayed him with a man whose memory she could not even recall? Terry looked up from his meal and catching her eye, his delight in her recovery shone from him and they exchanged smiles of acceptance of a shared past love that closed with an astonishing outcome that neither of them could have imagined. The happiness that Madeline brought him was clear to see and it eased her conscience.

A spark of memory, like a word on the tip of ones tongue, began to hover at the back of her mind. It was happening to her more and more these days, flashbacks of her life, catching her unawares. Her eyes lingered at the family table where Aunt Alice, home for the first time from Greece, was talking animatedly to Aunt Phoebe. Aunty May sensing Kitty's eyes upon them, lifted a plump hand and waved with a beaming smile. Kitty grinned back at her with a sweeping sense of love for her aunt who knew her as intimately as her mother, and was there as steadfast as a rock from the moment of her birth.

She suddenly became conscious of Verity sitting with them looking radiant in an outfit of blue and gold with a delightful froth of a wedding hat that Kitty remembered them buying together, trying this and that one on with laughter, and Verity thrilled at the thought of Kitty's forthcoming wedding. Her smile at Kitty seemed to light the room and she felt the warmth of Verity's love reaching out to her, until reality caused a shiver of cold goose bumps to shoot down her spine. She stared, telling herself it was a trick of her mind, a manifestation from her head trauma but Verity lingered, shining with an aura of happiness and joy until she gradually faded away.

Kitty slumped in her chair and there was a collective hush of dismay. Peter caught her and an alarmed Thomas threw back his chair and came to his aid.

'We must get Kitty out into the fresh air Thomas.'

A concerned young waiter ran ahead opening doors, and pulling up chairs in the hotel's entrance, they sat Kitty down and Peter held her head between her knees.

'She's just fainted,' Peter said, to an anxious Thomas. 'The room was hot and with the excitement of the wedding…..'

Kitty stirred and Peter helped her to sit up. 'How are you feeling, darling?'

'A bit weird.'

'You fainted, Kitty. If you sit quietly for a few minutes, you'll start to feel better.' The instinct of his training took over, checking her pulse and eyes, both were normal.

Octavia emerged from the reception room with a tearful Amy clinging to her hand.

'Thomas, if you could let everyone know Kitty is OK and to please carry on with their meal, I would be grateful. We shall be back at the reception soon,' said Peter.

'Are you sure she's well, Peter?' said Thomas, his voice betraying his anxiety.

'Absolutely.'

'But what caused her to faint? It's never happened before,' said Octavia with worry etched over her face.

'I think the heat. The weather's been exceptional,' replied Peter.

Amy ran to Kitty and burst into tears.

Kitty held out her arms to her. 'Oh Amy, don't cry, I just fainted, that's all. I'm feeling much better now.' She held her close and an echo of a memory that had been hovering on the edge of her consciousness became a picture of Amy tottering towards her, her fair hair shining in the sunlight, her arms outstretched to be picked up and swung around. Overcome at the memory of her baby daughter she gazed at Amy's face, seeing her as if for the first time since she was born. She looked up at Peter and Octavia, her eyes alight.

'I thought this would never happen. It has come back to me. I remember Amy as a baby. Isn't it wonderful?' she said, hugging Amy tightly to her.

'Oh darling, that's fantastic,' said Peter.

'And on your wedding day,' said Octavia, overjoyed. 'It couldn't have happened at a better time for you or Amy.'

Kitty's eyes returned to her daughter, eyes brimming with love.

'Just look at you. All grown up and looking so beautiful in your bridesmaid's dress. I've missed so much,' she said, with tears in her eyes.

With the speed children accept the fortunes of change, Amy's dejection evaporated. After so long waiting and hoping for this moment, happiness burst from her in a great ball of forgiving love.

'Don't cry mummy, it's not your fault. You've been very sick.'

'Yes, I know, but everything's going to be different now,' because I remember when you were born. You were such a beautiful baby, and now you've grown into my little girl that I love very much,' she said, stroking her hair and kissing her. 'You've been so good looking after me and now it's my turn to look after you and not be acting like a silly big sister!'

Amy giggled and Kitty vowed nothing would ever separate her again from the love of her daughter.

Amy looked at Octavia and her smile shone with the brilliance of a star. 'I'm *so* happy granny,' and with the honesty and a child's lack of guile said, 'mummy's not pretending any more that she loves me.'

Her words were hard to hear, leaving Kitty bereft and Octavia's joy dropping from her face.

Peter seeing them at a loss for words, said, 'You have always been very special to mummy Amy, and like she said, now her memory has returned, she can be your mother again like she always was before her accident. This is a day I don't think we shall ever forget will we?'

Amy shook her head. 'No! It's the bestest day of my *whole* life!' she said, excitedly.

'Now, I think it's time we all returned to the wedding, don't you?' said Peter, 'or our guests will think we've done a runner. You go ahead with granny, Amy, and we will follow you in a few minutes.'

He gave Octavia a reassuring look. 'I've checked Kitty over. She's fine, nothing to worry about at all.'

'Well if you're sure, in that case, we'll go on in. Come on Amy. We must get back and finish off our pudding. I hope the ice cream hasn't melted, don't you?' she said, resolutely keeping her tone light after Amy's heart breaking remark.

'And we have to keep a space for the wedding cake,' Amy said, floating on air to the reception, and turning her head back again and again to smile at Kitty.

As they disappeared Peter said jubilantly, 'Well, my beautiful bride didn't I say the best memories would return given time? We could not have wished for a more magnificent gift on our wedding day.'

'No, we couldn't.'

He studied her face. 'What's the matter, Kitty?' for he saw something else lay beneath her elation.

Kitty wavered.

Please tell me, darling. Whatever it is, I will understand.'

She began hesitantly. 'I know you're going to think I'm crazy….only….I saw Verity at the reception as clearly as I see you. She was smiling at me and looking so happy and real I thought she was alive, until I remembered she died a few weeks ago.'

'Kitty you're not crazy. What you've experienced is not unknown. I've come across it many times. It's a common phenomena people seeing or sensing their loved ones around them after they've died.'

'You don't know how much it means to hear you say that. Why did she have to die Peter?' Kitty cried out. One minute she was here and the next gone. I still can't believe it. We all loved her so much. It just isn't fair.'

'No, you're right. Life isn't very fair at times. An aneurism is silent and rapid and death can follow so quickly it makes it difficult for those left behind to accept. I'm so sorry it happened. I know how much she meant to you.'

'She saved my life. She was there for me the whole time I was in hospital. I can even remember her voice when I was in a coma saying "You will get better and I shall take you home." And she did.' Kitty paused, thinking about her time in Nancarrow, and decided she should speak of it. She owed him that at least.

'Peter there's something else I've wanted to tell you. It happened when I was in Nancarrow. I was sitting outside on the terrace enjoying the sunshine when I went back in time to the garden like it was when I was a child. I heard her voice again whispering in my ear, '*I am here, I am always with you.*' It was my guardian angel. They say identical twins are exceptionally close, don't they, and I think my twin never left me, and has been protecting me all my life. She saved me from drowning once.'

'Yes, Aunty May told me the story.'

Kitty looked at him in surprise. 'Did she? Well Aunty May was always more open to the idea of the supernatural. Mum thinks its all madness. My ways are a complete mystery to her! You don't think I'm mad too, do you?' afraid she had said too much.

To her amazement Peter laughed. 'Kitty, you've been as mad as a hatter from the minute I set eyes on you! It's the reason I love you so much and nothing will ever change that.'

Kitty laughed with him in relief. He understood her as no-one else did. She stood up from the chair. 'Well, now that I know what you *really* think of me, perhaps we'd better go back in before you change your mind!'

He grinned at her and checked his inside pocket of his wedding jacket for his piece of paper with the bullet points for the most important speech of his life. Yes, it was there. He took Kitty into his arms.

'Well, Mrs. Edwards are you up for the rest of our lives together?'

'More than you'll ever know,' she said softly, loving him man and boy.

She was home.

ACKNOWLEDGEMENTS

A number of fellow scribes and friends inspired and supported me in the writing of this book.

I would like to thank -

Georgina Russell for her guidance on nursing procedures and for the fun and enthusiastic encouragement.

Wendy Carter, Judith Hamilton, Diane Simkin, Hazel Penhaligon and Jeff George for their suggestions and for sharing war-time memories with me.

Patti Hopgood for being there at the end of a line and lifting my spirits.

Enid Mavor for patiently proof reading my first manuscript.

Pat Limberg who first saw a book in me and set me on the path to writing it.

Sean Croft and his artistic eye in designing the striking book cover.

Terry Lander, my understanding publisher and his wife Mary who kindly read and offered feedback and corrections on the final draft of my book.

And for family and friends for their love and belief that the sequel would finally come to fruition.

Any war-time or medical inaccuracies are mine alone.

ABOUT THE AUTHOR

Katie-Louise Merritt was born and raised in Camborne, Cornwall. On her marriage, she lived in West Africa and Malaysia. In 1972 she returned to England and now lives in Cornwall near her family and grandchildren.

Articles and cameos of her childhood have featured in local publications under her married name of Kathryn Garrod and her poems winning recognition in competitions have been widely published.

A collection of her poetry, *The Voice That Calls*, came out in 2001 and her first novel, *Where Shadows Lie*, was published in 2009.